CRJ

VOYAGE TO THE VOLCANO

Being a continuation of
the telling of the voyages,
mishaps and triumphs of
Captain Meredith Anstruther,
his crew and his celebrated
Great Galloon.

TOM BANKS

First published in Great Britain in 2013 by Hot Key Books
Northburgh House, 10 Northburgh Street, London EC1V 0AT

A CIP catalogue record for this book is available from the British Library.

ISBN: 978-1-4714-0170-1

1

Typeset by Palimpsest Book Production Limited, Falkirk, Stirlingshire
This book is set in 11.75 pt Sabon LT Std

Printed and bound by Clays Ltd, St Ives Plc

FSC

Hot Key Books supports the Forest Stewardship Council (FSC), the leading
international forest certification organisation, and is committed to printing
only on Greenpeace-approved FSC-certified paper.

www.hotkeybooks.com

Hot Key Books is part of the Bonnier Publishing Group
www.bonnierpublishing.com

For Ma and Pa B – and all the other magnanimous
baby boomers who've helped along the way

Dear Reader,

Throughout these stories of 'The Great Galloon' you will find goodnight points. Please be aware that these are the author's suggestion only. If you are reading this story to yourself, please feel free to keep on reading until the sun comes up and you have to go to school, work, court, space, etc. If you are reading these stories to someone else, then you may place the Goodnight points wherever you see fit, as long as permission is obtained in writing from the author, both of his parents, and his old English teacher Mr Foster.

Voyage to the Volcano

It was always chilly on the deck of the Great Galloon. Despite the braziers burning, temperatures never seemed to reach much above nippy, rising to parky in places. It was chilly because the Galloon spent most of its time miles up in the sky, where the air is very thin indeed. But today it was different. Today it was *really* cold.

The Galloon was encrusted with ice – the rigging was brittle with it, the sails were heavy with it, and the decks were so shiny with it that they had the look of expensive pieces of furniture, polished up for a vicar's visit. For today the Great Galloon, the fantastical and gargantuan craft of Captain Meredith Anstruther, was further north and higher in the sky than it had been for a long time.

Stanley and Rasmussen were sitting on top of the

1

huge figurehead, right at the front of the gigantic vessel. His name was Claude, and he was a winged tiger of immense size. Legend had it that if the Galloon or its Captain were ever in mortal peril Claude would fly to the rescue, but then legend had a lot of things that were clearly nonsense. Stanley knew that the Galloon had been in mortal peril more times than anyone could remember, and yet Claude remained in his place, wings outstretched, mouth open, a danger only to the occasional pigeon that didn't get out of the way in time. But his head made a magnificent viewing platform, if you were brave enough to clamber out over the rail from the main deck, which of course Stanley was, with a little coaxing from his good friend, Rasmussen.

Holding onto one ear each, they craned to see the landscape scooting by below them. Jutting from the clouds only a few hundred metres away, were rocky crags, razor-sharp cliffs, and snow-capped summits like the teeth of a world-eating shark. The Galloon was skimming along, at a fair old rate of knots, above the highest and coldest mountain range for many thousands of miles around – the fabled Eisberg Mountains.

'And that must be Castle Eisberg!' cried Rasmussen, her voice just carrying to where Stanley stood, before the wind whipped it away. She was nodding her head and pointing with her eyebrows towards a crag on the mountainside.

Stanley squinted. After a moment he glimpsed a green turret, which almost immediately disappeared in the cloud. Then a tumbledown tower revealed itself, still a long way off, before disappearing again. The ringing of a distant bell told them that someone down there had probably seen them too. Still clinging to Claude's huge wooden ear, Stanley leaned forward, to peer more closely.

'It's quite . . . small,' he said thoughtfully. A stretch of crumbling crenellations appeared, before sinking into the fog again, as if the world-eating shark was diving for the hunt.

'And quite . . . broken,' said Rasmussen, also leaning forward dangerously.

'Hmmm. I can see two people running around on top. What's that they've got?' mused Stanley, almost to himself.

'A caber?' said Rasmussen. 'A huge fencepost? A tree trunk?'

They watched through gaps in the clouds, as tiny figures seemed to be manoeuvring a long, heavy object around on the castle battlements.

'A big stick?' said Stanley. 'A gigantic pencil?'

By now both of them were leaning so far forward that they were on tiptoes, with only Claude and the clouds below them.

'Here we go,' said Rasmussen. 'Something's happening.

They seem to have it where they want it, and a flash has come out the end. Some kind of firework perhaps?'

'Cannonball,' said Stanley calmly, as the object flashed again.

'Don't be silly. It's much too big and long to be a cannonball. It's more like a cannon, if anything. Oh, I see.'

Stanley was now pointing with one hand, while clinging onto Claude with the other.

'Cannonball,' he said again thoughtfully.

Way below and in front of the Galloon, a tiny round object was creating a vortex as it whipped through the clouds. Rasmussen peered even harder, and Stanley heard her say, 'Ooooh yeeeah,' under her breath in a kind of mildly interested way, before the whole world tipped up.

There was a noise like a tree snapping, and Stanley wrapped both legs around Claude's ear, as the whole Galloon pitched sharply to the right. Or did it? Turning frantically to see what had caused the movement, it seemed to Stanley that the rail round the Galloon's foredeck stayed level with the horizon, which was odd.

Still clinging on, Stanley turned to Rasmussen, to remark on this strange turn of events, and to express his hope that this silly cannonball business wouldn't get in the way of a good adventure. But his words never came. He saw Rasmussen grasping for Claude's ear, as she tried desperately to keep her balance. For a few seconds, she was untethered, surfing through the clouds on a huge tiger's head, with a manic grin on her face, before the wind took her coat. She lost her balance, and tumbled backwards into the empty air.

Stanley heard her shout, 'Weeee!' as she went.

'Rasmusseeeen!' he shouted, slightly self-consciously. He stared dumbly at the place where she had been, by Claude's enormous wooden ear. It seemed to flicker as Stanley blinked back tears. There was a noise that sounded like 'poot', as if a giant wooden tiger was spitting out a red-hot cannonball. And then there was just the wind.

GOODNIGHT!

Many decks below, in one of the Galloon's map rooms, Captain Anstruther was pouring coffee and poring over charts of the Eisberg Mountains.

'Descending, three hundred feet per minute, yawing left eight degrees,' he muttered.

'Erm . . .' said Clamdigger, the lanky cabin boy and

general factotum on the Galloon, who was standing by the door ready to be useful. He held up a finger as if testing the wind, before remembering he was indoors.

'I could check for you, sir?' he suggested.

'What?' said the Captain, looking up at him with red-rimmed eyes. 'No, no. No need, thank yer, Clam. Wasn't asking, as it happens. We must be over Castle Eisberg now, near as nuts, so we'll be getting ready to moor up.' And he went back to looking at the chart in front of him. Clamdigger had been craning his neck to see which chart it was, and which bit of it was holding the Captain's attention, but from where he stood he could only make out contour lines and blue shading.

'Odd little jolt there, though. And she feels a fraction out of kilter,' said the Captain in the same distracted tone. 'Any ideas?'

Clamdigger knew better than to interrupt his train of thought a second time, so he stood where he was and waited. The Captain looked tired, his cheeks greyer, his eyes redder than before. He had always been a slightly distant figure, but nowadays he restricted himself to the odd enquiry about the Galloon's welfare, and very little else. Two months had passed since the Captain's brother Zebediah had made off with his beautiful young bride-to-be, and in that time the Captain had lost a good deal of weight, although none of his imposing presence. Clamdigger risked a look at the Captain, who was still bent over his charts, but quickly snapped his gaze back to the middle distance when the Captain spoke again.

'Any ideas, I say?' he said, at which point Clamdigger realised the question was not rhetorical, but aimed at him.

'Oh, err. A loose sheet? Bird strike? Turbulence?' he said.

'Hmm. Could be,' rumbled the Captain, obviously unconvinced.

'Cosmic dust? Raiders? Ice on the rigging?' said Clamdigger, grinding to a halt.

'Felt like . . . but no,' said Captain Anstruther. 'No doubt someone will tell me in good time. Ah!'

This last word was said with a slight smile of satisfaction, but before Clamdigger could wonder why, the door handle beside him began to rattle as someone tried to open it. It wasn't locked, but it was stiff, so Clamdigger lent a hand from the inside. As he did so, the door burst open, and a stick-thin figure in a sky-blue uniform burst through, tripped over his own feet, and grabbed hold of the nearest object to steady himself.

Unfortunately, the nearest object was a tray of decanters which had been set on the huge map table that dominated the room. The new arrival, still unbalanced, found himself trying to counterbalance this surprising new addition to his person. He teetered about the room for a few moments, emitting quiet woohoos of surprise, before Clamdigger stepped in and whipped the tray off him. Thus unencumbered, Able Skyman Abel, for it was he, grabbed the back of a tall chair and righted himself at last. He looked urgently about, then glared at Clamdigger.

'A cheap trick, Master Clamdigger. I would expect better of you. But I was, as ever, one step ahead.'

'I was trying . . .' began Clamdigger, but Abel had already turned smartly on a heel to face the Captain.

'Cannonball, was it?' said the Captain.

'Sir, I have to report that at seven hundred hours ack emma . . . oh. Yes, sir, a cannonball.'

'Perhaps the Count has not completely forgiven me, as I'd hoped,' said the Captain, still staring intently at his charts.

'Forgiven you, sir? I thought you were old school pals?' said Abel.

'Oh, we are. Sat together every day for twelve years. Inseparable, we were. And later on I was his best man, you know. But, also there has been animosity on occasion.' said the Captain, still not looking up.

'Animosity?' said Clamdigger, to another glare from Abel. 'I thought that was saved for . . .'

'Zebediah?' said the Captain. 'Yes. It's time the Count and I put our differences behind us. It all seems a bit silly now.'

'What's the Count of Eisberg got to forgive you for, anyway?' asked Clamdigger.

'I don't think we need to go into that at the moment, Jack,' said Abel, using Clamdigger's first name, as he did when he wanted to seem fatherly. 'The Captain doesn't want to share his life story with a bloomin' cabin boy.'

The Captain shifted awkwardly in his seat, and looked between them.

'So,' he said. 'Any damage done? By this cannonball?'

Abel jumped to attention. 'No, sir – that's the thing. We tracked it on its way up here, then it just seemed to disappear, sir. Just at the point when it should have hit. Somewhere around the bows. Ms Huntley is on her way to conduct an inspection, but we've heard no reports of any damage done. Very odd.'

'The bows, you say?' said the Captain. 'Hmm. Everyone accounted for?'

'Of course! I'd soon hear if anyone went overboard,' said Abel. 'All present and correct, and if so-called Count Whatsisname tries his cannonball trick again we'll be ready for him. By gosh, we'll . . .'

But Clamdigger didn't hear what Abel planned to do. With a huge crash, a red-hot cannonball smashed through the window. It screamed across the room, spun the Captain's hat round on his head, ricocheted off a battered suit of armour, and embedded itself in the oaken table. The decanters that Abel had worked so hard to save fell to the floor, where they joined the broken window glass strewn across the boards. Abel screamed a high C-sharp, and Clamdigger ducked behind the door. The Captain hauled himself from his seat, righted his hat and took a sip of coffee.

'You were wrong about the cannonball,' he said to Abel, as a look of amazement crossed his face. 'And you were wrong about the crew. Look!'

They ran to the window and, there, hanging by the hood of her coat from one of Claude's enormous outstretched claws, was Rasmussen. Her hair was streaming out behind her, and her face was set in a rictus grin. Icicles were forming on her teeth. Abel stammered. The Captain boomed. Clamdigger ran to the suit of armour, and grabbed the pikestaff from its fist. With this fearsome weapon in his hands, he turned carefully, and poked all eleven feet of it out through the empty window frame. The Captain grabbed the staff as it came past him, and together they tried to move it into a position from where Rasmussen could safely grab it and be pulled back onboard.

'Hold on, my girl!' said Abel weakly as he stood watching the Captain and Clamdigger's attempts. Neither Clamdigger nor the Captain spoke. Clamdigger noticed from the corner of his eye that the Captain's

11

tongue was sticking out, and he had one eye closed. He wondered vaguely why people did this when they were trying to concentrate, before realising that he was doing it too. Now Rasmussen had seen them, and she was watching the end of the staff waggle around in thin air a few feet from her face, but she was clearly too cold and terrified to move anything more than her eyes.

'The coat, lad . . . hook . . . the coat . . .' said the Captain through gritted teeth, as he leaned back with the very end of the staff under his armpit.

'No!' called Abel from behind them. 'The dress! More sturdy – the coat's only done up with toggles, a very unsound fastening!'

The Captain and Clamdigger looked at each other and nodded in agreement. Clamdigger leaned as far out of the window as he dared. The air was bitterly cold, and it stung his eyes as he squinted hard, desperate not to lose sight of Rasmussen for one moment. The staff was now close to her, but dipping too low. The Captain had his feet braced on the window frame either side of Clamdigger, who was using all of his wiry strength to bring it up to Rasmussen's level so they could hook her free, or she could grab on, or . . . what? He wasn't really sure, but they had to keep trying.

'Up a bit!' squeaked Abel, leaning transfixed from the next window.

The Captain made a noise that may have been a

grunt of effort, or may have been a growl. Clamdigger redoubled his efforts, and finally had the far end, the sharp end, of the pikestaff waggling around just inches below Rasmussen's dangling feet.

'Can't get it . . . any higher . . . Cap'n,' he said over his shoulder. As he did so, Rasmussen let out a squeal that was most unlike her.

'Drop, girl!' shouted the Captain, and Clamdigger heard Abel let out a squeal of his own.

'We'll catch you!' the Captain continued, bellowing at the top of his mighty lungs. 'And if we don't, Claude will!'

Clamdigger had no time to wonder what this meant. With his tongue still sticking out, and his arms now feeling as if they were about to snap in two, he watched in awe as Rasmussen looked down at the waving bill-hook below her, and then up at Claude's mighty claw. She reached up oh so carefully, and Clamdigger's heart was in his mouth as he saw her trying to rip the hood of her fleece-lined parka – the only thing keeping her up here, in the freezing air over the jagged peaks of a hostile mountain range. She tugged, and then she tugged again. The hood held fast. To Clamdigger's streaming eyes, it seemed as if there was a slight flicker, and then Rasmussen was falling. Clamdigger closed his eyes, gripped the pikestaff even tighter and lunged.

*　　*　　*

Stanley was making good progress. When Rasmussen had first disappeared into thin air, he had done the first thing that the situation seemed to demand – he had stared blankly at the place where she had been, and done a little laugh.

'Haha!' he had said, just after he had said, 'Rasmusseeeen!'

But then he had sprung into action. He had crept from Claude's head, clambered over the rail, and hailed the nearest Galloonier. Together they had raised the alarm, and now the whole for'ard section of the Galloon was abustle. Rescue parties and life balloons were being launched, and bells were clanging as Stanley ran to find the Captain, or Ms Huntley, or someone who could stop the Galloon's progress and co-ordinate the rescue. He had negotiated seven flights of stairs, two fireman's poles, a hand-cranked freight lift and a wooden cargo chute just to get onto the right deck, and even then he had been hundreds of yards away from his destination, but now he was running down the corridor that led to the Captain's map room, with Gallooniers shouting directions and encouragement as he went. An old hand called Tarheel, who was running the other way with a length of rope in his arms, turned as Stanley passed him.

'Never lost a man yet!' he said, with a forced grin.

Yes, thought Stanley, *but Rasmussen is not a man.* His heart was beating in his throat as he approached the door to the map room. Surely the Captain wouldn't ignore this situation as he had ignored the recent affair of the all-consuming monster moths until the last possible moment? He stood before the brass plate that said 'Here Be Mappes', and composed himself. It was easy to tell yourself that onboard the Galloon, nothing could ever truly go wrong, but of course this was not the case. Stanley swallowed hard, and knocked.

'Come in!' said a sonorous voice within, so Stanley opened the door a crack. There was the Captain, as awe-inspiring as ever, sitting at the head of the green baize map table, scrutinising a huge map of the Eisberg Mountains. Beside him stood Able Skyman Abel, who seemed to be inspecting a dent in the Captain's enormous hat. As Stanley stepped into the room, he noticed that the freezing wind was whistling in through broken windows, and broken glass crunched underfoot. A large iron ball was embedded in the wood of the table, which was smoking with the heat that came from it. Behind the table, Clamdigger was standing and smiling. Beside him, sitting in a leather-backed chair, toasting a crumpet in the heat from the cannonball, was Rasmussen. She looked dishevelled but happy, and as Stanley came in, she gave him her trademark infuriating wink.

'Hello, slowcoach,' she said. At this, Able Skyman Abel looked up at Stanley and frowned.

'Ah, Sidney,' he said. 'I imagine you've come to tell

15

us of this young lady's mishap. But fear not – I . . . er . . . we had the situation in hand throughout. Kindly run along and report to Ms Huntley that our little escapee is safely back onboard, and that the bells can cease to clang. The Captain is trying to concentrate. Best tell Her Grace the Countess as well, so she can start getting young madam ready for the ball. Hurry up, lad, no time for slouching and gawping.'

'Yes,' said Rasmussen, stuffing crumpet into her mouth and swinging her feet up onto the table. 'Hurry along, Sidney, there's a good chap.'

Back on deck a short while later, Stanley was trying to stay out of the way as he watched the loose conglomeration of people that made up the crew of the Great Galloon working together as only they could. Having not grown up onboard, Stanley still didn't take for granted the fact that everyone on the Galloon was there of their own free will, under no obligation, and free to do as they pleased.

The fact that what it pleased them all to do was to work together for the Galloon's greater good was testament to the loyalty that Captain Anstruther inspired in all who knew him.

Stanley was huddled in his scarf and gloves, tucked in beside the Galloon's main funnel. At this hour the funnel was warm with the smoke coming up from the

16

great furnace, and so this was the prime spot on deck. He watched as a gang of wiry old hands erected netting all around the Galloon, to minimise any damage from future cannonballs. He heard a far-off clatter, which he knew to be the anchor crews lowering the mighty ice anchors, and he felt that familiar glow of satisfaction that came with being part of such a magnificent thing as the Galloon.

As Stanley sat watching the hustle and bustle all around him, he heard a noise – a whistle and a whoosh together, like a firework. Beyond the netting, in the snow-burgeoning sky, a flare of some sort exploded, and a shower of dark grey ash spread out across the clouds. Stanley was interested but not shocked, until the cloud of ash began to form itself into recognisable words. In a firm Teutonic hand, the firework writing relayed its message to the Captain, and by extension all aboard the Great Galloon:

My birthday ball is cancelled due to too much interest. Please leave. We apologise for any inconvenience caused. Eisberg.

And then the ashen words fell apart and drifted to earth. Stanley was confused.

'*Too much* interest?' he said to himself, and jumped when a voice beside him responded.

'Poppycock!' said Clamdigger, who had appeared, to warm his long fingers on the funnel. 'The Captain will have something to say about that.'

And indeed he did – far behind them on the quarterdeck, his great hat framed against the white sky, his mouth to the huge brass speaking trumpet, rigged up to tubes around the ship for just such moments as these, the Captain spoke to his crew.

'Poppycock!' he said. 'We've come for a ball, and by hook or by crook a ball we shall have. It is imperative. Gallooniers, prepare a landing party – Ms Peele and Her Grace the Countess, in the first instance, I think.'

A ragged cheer sprung up in the rigging, and was then taken up across the ship. Stanley was surprised at the force of the Captain's words. He didn't cheer, being lost in thought as he so often was.

Corks, he thought. *Perhaps this is the start of that adventure we've been waiting for . . .*

And with that thought on his mind, he scratched his horn, blew on his hands, and strode off to find his best friend Rasmussen.

A short while later, Cloudier Peele was carefully piloting her weather balloon, bringing it alongside the Galloon amidships, where the boatswain's chair was hanging from its derrick. The weather balloon was a tiny, simple craft, one small basket hung beneath one small balloon.

Cloudier had only been given full use of it relatively recently, and manoeuvres like this were new to her. She had in one gloved hand a light rope attached to a leather flap in the top curve of the balloon, which could be used to let air out, and in the other a brass knob, which controlled the flame of a small burner. Right hand down, left hand up. Simple.

But Cloudier was a poet at heart, not a navigator like her mother. She couldn't help thinking of the poetic possibilities – a young girl drifting off into the sky, out of control in her tiny craft, to wander the world alone. Or plummeting to earth in a desperate fireball, having time only to scribble a line or two in her charred notebook before icy waters claimed her. Having a poet's mind was a pain sometimes. She dragged her attention back to the more prosaic situation at hand.

At the moment, a squat Galloonier called Tamp was fending her off from the side of the Galloon with a long boathook, while stopping her drifting away by means of a stout length of rope wrapped round his waist. Every once in a while he shouted things like 'Easy now!' or 'Bring her along!', but Cloudier just did her best to stay level, and he seemed happy enough with this. She was waiting for the shore party to board, when it would be her job to take them down to Castle Eisberg, in an attempt to find out what was going on. In the meantime, she was standing braced against the edge of the basket, trying not to show the effort involved in piloting the balloon, and squinting at the coffee table by her feet, on which a small poetry anthology was held open with stones.

Cloudier had, in the last few weeks, made an astounding discovery. She loved poetry. Not just the idea of it, she genuinely loved it. Her favourite book, once well thumbed but never read, had finally been devoured, and then studied, and then memorised, and now it was little more than a loose collection of leaves held together with string. She couldn't get enough, from tumpty-tumpty doggerel to epic verse, from limericks to haikus to sonnets and back again. She was still writing her own poems, and planned to give a recital as part of the ball, if the Count was amenable, so she was very much hoping the landing party could persuade him to get over his last-minute jitters and declare the ball back on. Something about the mountains, she thought. An homage to their majesty, their steadfastness, their kindly eyes and stripy jumper.

'What?' she said aloud, confused by her own train of thought, and then realised that Clamdigger was speaking to her. He was standing at the rail of the Galloon, with a small two-note whistle in his hand.

'I said, prepare for boarding, weather balloon there!'
said Clamdigger, and he blew a little fanfare on his
whistle.

Cloudier laughed awkwardly, then stopped. She
accidentally let the rope slip through her right hand
for a moment, and so Clamdigger seemed from her
viewpoint to fly quickly up into the air. She regained
control, and used the burner to float gracefully back
into his eye line. She cleared her throat, and called
back.

'T—' she said, at the exact same moment that he
began to speak, so she missed what he said. He stared
at her, and spoke again. So did she.

'Pr—' they said together. Cloudier coloured up, but
managed another little laugh.

Giving up on speech, Clamdigger blew his whistle
again, a complicated two-note trill, which meant
'landing party preparing to leave the Galloon', although
only he and Abel would know that. He then spoke
quietly to Tamp, who braced himself hard against the
rail, putting most of his weight into holding the weather
balloon steady alongside. Unseen hands must then have
brought a long gang plank into place, for Cloudier saw
one rise up behind Clamdigger, swing high over his
head, then float precariously out into space, before
coming to rest on the edge of the weather balloon.

Gritting her teeth with concentration, Cloudier kept

21

the balloon dead level as two lithe crew members leapt over the rail and began to erect a rope handrail along the edge of the gangplank, setting banister posts into sockets along its edge, and slinging yet another rope between them, for all the world as if they weren't standing in the icy clouds, with nothing but a bowing plank and the untried skills of a teenage girl between them and the long drop.

Job done, they saluted her unnecessarily, and slipped back over the rail onto the Galloon itself. Two more toots on the whistle, and into Cloudier's view hove a vision of elegance – the Dowager Countess of Hammerstein in full sail, tiara aloft, jewels glinting despite the fog, beshawled and muffed, with a steely look in her beautiful eyes as she stepped undaunted onto the gangplank.

'Hello, Cloudier,' she said as she came into the balloon, for all the world as if she was strolling through the park on a Sunday afternoon.

'Hello, Your Grace,' said Cloudier, who had known the Countess for many years.

'It seems that the Captain is very keen indeed to attend the Eisberg winter ball,' said the Countess, almost to herself. 'And for some reason, he believes that I am the person to persuade the Count to go ahead with it. So let us descend and see what can be done.'

'Of course,' said Cloudier.

The Countess deftly untied the knot connecting the gangplank to the basket's edge, and with one gloved finger in her mouth, whistled so loudly that Cloudier's ears rang. An answering whistle came from beyond the rail, and hands once again unseen began to haul in the plank.

Craning only slightly to see whether Clamdigger was still watching, Cloudier let some air out of the balloon in a controlled fashion, and they began their descent through the swirls of mist, to the mysterious castle.

A short while later down below, Stanley was still looking for Rasmussen. He had checked back in the map room, and not finding her there, had tried Rasmussen's own chambers, where she lived with the Dowager Countess. A neighbour had told him they were both out, so he had tried some friends' cabins, and the toyshop, but with no sign of her. The for'ard games room, the starboard library, the ballroom and the top bakery had all felt like good ideas at the time, but to no avail. So he had hitched a ride on a passing dog cart, and taken in the long gallery, Dobson's folly, the town-hall steps, and all along Conduit Way. These were all their usual haunts, but she was nowhere to be found.

Clicking his tongue and rolling his eyes, he had ridden a dumb waiter up to the refectory, but Snivens the butler hadn't seen her all day. Beginning to get cross, he had even tried the school room, where Rasmussen was barely known, but of course she wasn't there. So here he was, almost out of ideas, standing outside the Captain's cabin once again. He raised a fist, and was just about to knock, when he heard voices inside.

'I've never known you so worked up about a party before, Captain,' said a voice that Stanley recognised as that of Ms Huntley, the navigator.

'Blast the party to Easter and back,' said the Captain. 'I couldn't care a hoot for the party.'

'Well, I think the Gallooniers could do with blowing off a bit of steam after recent events,' said Ms Huntley, apparently unbowed by his snappy tone.

'Recent events?' asked the Captain.

'I'm referring to our almost being eaten alive by monster moths, just a few weeks back. Not to mention the subsequent attack by the Berbers of Seveell, and that incident with the escaped chimera.' Ms Huntley sounded concerned, but firm. 'The crew needs a rest. And so do you.'

'I won't be mollycoddled, Ms Huntley,' said the Captain firmly. 'Thank you for your kindness, but I'm not some stray lamb that needs warming by the fire.'

'Far be it from me to suggest otherwise,' said Ms Huntley, with what sounded to Stanley like the merest hint of impatience in her voice. 'But if you couldn't give a hoot for the Count's birthday party, why have you sent Her Grace the Dowager Countess of Hammerstein, of all people, to persuade the Count not to cancel it?

'He won't see me, not while he's all worked up,' said the Captain. 'We have history, the Count and I. We've been friends since we were boys, shared a dorm at school, and then went through service together. But we've had our fallings out of late.'

'What kind of fallings out?' said Stanley to himself, outside the door, just as Ms Huntley said the same thing inside.

'It may be – just may be, you understand – that my darling Isabella, love of my life, was once sworn unto him.'

Stanley heard Ms Huntley gasp.

'One o' these family matches you understand – the way the nobility will make a match without either party knowing the other. Organised by their parents, with no input from the Count or Isabella.'

'So you . . . stole her away from him?' said Ms H, in a measured tone.

'No,' said the Captain firmly. 'Neither of them wanted it – but still, when Isabella and I met and fell in love, it wasn't quite seen as the done thing.'

'But . . . surely, you saved them both from a life of unhappiness?' said Ms Huntley sympathetically.

'Perhaps. But whether he sees it that way, I've never stuck around to find out.'

'I need Birgit to persuade the Count to have that party. Our fates depend on it.'

'Well,' said Ms Huntley, and Stanley was alarmed to hear she was approaching the door. 'If anyone can persuade him, Birgit can.'

Stanley was confused by all this, but he just had enough of his wits about him to jump out of the way as the door opened and Ms Huntley came out.

'Let's hope so . . .' called the Captain from inside. 'For all our sakes.'

Ms Huntley closed the door behind her and looked inquisitively at Stanley, who was now standing in the corridor with his hands over his eyes.

'Ninety-seven, ninety-eight, ninety-nine . . . one hundred!' he said, and took his hands away from his face. 'Coming, ready or not!' he called, and then pretended to notice Ms Huntley.

'Oh, hello,' he said. 'I'm just playing backgammon.'

And with that he ran away.

*   *   *

27

In a wood-panelled room, a face looked out of a mirror. It was a plain face, male, of indeterminate age. The kind of face that went with the phrase 'no distinguishing features'. The owner of the face had no strong feelings about it, but knew it was the perfect face for his trade.

Arranged between the face and the mirror was an array of little objects that would have looked to an observer like children's playthings. A wig, some glue, a rubber nose, some make-up. The face's owner didn't think of them as playthings. He thought of them as tools. Metaphorically, he picked up a hammer and chisel, and began to chip away at the featureless marble block of his face. He knew, as he always did, that something astounding would emerge . . .

Cloudier's heart was still racing from the excitement of the journey down to Castle Eisberg, but she was doing her best not to show it. She had struggled to keep on course through the thick fog, but at least the air had been still, and the castle was quite a big target.

It seemed that the inhabitants had either run out of ammunition, or hadn't seen them coming, because they had landed uncontested in a messy courtyard, slap in the middle of the castle. The courtyard, and indeed the hillside all around the castle, was filled with vehicles, animals and entourages of all sorts. From lowly pony carts to huge ornate coaches, from sedan chairs to steamcars, all forms of transport were there. Footmen lounged, chauffeurs chatted, cabbies snoozed under their great furry cloaks – it was clear to Cloudier that the Galloon was not the only vessel that had not been put off by the Count's automated messages.

She was secretly pleased with her piloting skills – she'd never taken the weather balloon away from the Galloon before, but she and the Countess had managed the journey and the difficult landing with no more damage than a bent weathervane and a startled sheep to show for it. They climbed out of the balloon – the Countess managing to maintain her graceful demeanour even while clambering over the side of the basket, which impressed Cloudier not a little. The drivers, grooms and chairpeople standing around in the court-yard were clearly impressed as well. A hush descended as the Countess made her stately way across the court-yard to the nearest door, while Cloudier trotted to keep up. The Countess took all this in her stride, as she always did, offering a cheery wave or a polite 'hello' to anyone they passed.

'Hello, Charlie,' she said to a smart, rosy-cheeked man in a peaked cap and a black suit. 'How are your chilblains?'

'Murder, ma'am, thanks for asking. Absolute ruddy murder,' said the man with a smile.

'Here, this may help,' said the Countess, handing Charlie a small bottle of lotion from her clutch bag. 'Keep it, keep it, I have more.'

'Th'ky, m'm,' mumbled Charlie, colouring up as the Countess folded his fingers over the tiny bottle. But the Countess had moved on.

'Carozza, how lovely to see you again. Chancellor Urquell is well, I presume?' She was now talking to a tall woman sitting on the running board of a sleek red carriage. 'Oh gosh, don't stand up!'

'You'll see for yourself, Miss Birgit,' said the tall woman pleasantly. 'She's inside, a-waiting on the Count to make himself known.'

'Aha. He is keeping a low profile, then?' said the Countess, and Cloudier noticed a lot of eyebrow raising in the people nearby.

'I should say so, ma'am,' said a bright-eyed lad on a shaggy pony. 'Sounds from out here like he's gone to ground. Not exactly the party of the century, shall we say!'

Ragged laughter broke out around Cloudier and the Countess, but it soon died down when the Countess did not join in.

'Hmmm. Poor Heinz. Shall we see if we can offer any help, Cloudier? I'm sure the situation just needs

30

looking at a different way,' said the Countess, moving on again, towards a postern door set in the base of a crumbling tower nearby.

'The Count needs his brain looking at a different way more like it!' said a raucous voice from across the courtyard.

The wag broke into croaking laughter at his own joke, until he realised that no one else was laughing, and that the Countess was watching him with interest, one perfect eyebrow raised. He turned his laugh into a cough, and his cough into an apology. Then he sat down heavily in the mud, gazing adoringly back at her. Cloudier stifled a chuckle, which she managed to turn into a tut, before rolling her eyes resignedly and following the Countess to the door.

The Countess knocked quietly, but it was clear that it was up to them to let themselves in. Inside, was a largish round room, in the base of the tumbledown tower. Across the circle from Cloudier, wooden steps, patched and cracked, led up to a gantry. On the gantry stood two guards, one with a lance in his hand, one plucking half-heartedly at a mandolin, each staring at nothing with a steely determination. And they needed that determination, for many, many people were trying to get their attention, and each of those people seemed to think their plea was more important than anyone else's. Dozens of people were clamouring to be allowed through the door behind the guards, where the Count of Eisberg presumably awaited. There were more pearls, opera glasses and fur stoles in this room than Cloudier had ever seen assembled before, and it seemed that the people wearing them each thought that such accoutrements entitled them to be heard first.

A lanky man in a deerstalker was haranguing one of the guards, but his accent was so refined that to Cloudier he sounded like a drunken bloodhound baying at the moon. A woman who had apparently forgotten to remove the previous owner from her fur coat was proclaiming to everyone that she could trace her ancestors back three thousand years, which from the look of her took her back to about her seventh birthday. A plum-coloured man with more medals than teeth was recounting his part in some battle, or perhaps he was telling people about a dream he had had – Cloudier found it hard to tell and harder to care. The overall impression she got was of a roomful of people who were used to getting their own way, and who thought that manners were for servants. Cloudier's stomach lurched as she heard a man shout, 'Do you know who you're talking to?' at one of the guards, but she was pleased to see that the guard did not respond.

Beside her, the Countess took a deep breath and began to move. Like an icebreaker swishing through the floe, she seemed untroubled by the throng. People moved aside as she came through, without her having to say anything except the occasional quiet 'excuse me'. Cloudier stayed close, knowing that the crowd would close up tight behind. As she moved, she heard the timbre of the noise in the room around her change. The indignant crowing of the entitled died down, and a kind of hissing murmur took its place.

'That's Hammerstein!' Cloudier heard.

'From the Galloon!'

'He must be nearby!'

'How uncouth, to send a countess to do the work of a mere captain . . .'

Cloudier would have responded to this last one, but she bumped into the Countess's bustle, as she had stopped at the foot of the rotten, sawdust-strewn stairs. The Countess put a gloved hand to her mouth.

'Excuse me, sir?' she called politely to the nearest guard. 'Is the Count quite well? Is there anything we can do to help?'

The nearest guard had been watching her from the corner of his eye as she made her way across the room, and Cloudier was not surprised to see that he appeared to be too tongue-tied to reply. But the second guard unrolled a scroll, and with barely a glance at it, declaimed the following prepared statement:

'His Grace the Count of Eisberg is currently experiencing a very high volume of visits. You have been placed in a queue, and will be answered as soon as possible. Thank you for your patience.'

Then he picked up his mandolin again and continued to play the plinky-plonky, music-free tune, with a glassy look in his eye.

'Oh dear, no,' said the Countess. 'This is worse than I feared.'

'There's nothing I can do, Countess,' said the mandolin-playing guard. 'Please be assured your visit is important to us.'

Cloudier noticed for the first time that this guard seemed more nervous than the other. The hands that plucked the mandolin were steady enough, but he was shaking at the knees, and sweat beaded on his lip beneath his thin moustache. She stared further, and saw that his armour didn't fit anywhere – the breast plate was for a much fatter man, the helmet was perched on top of his head like an eggcup, and the boots didn't even match. The other guard, in contrast, was quite well turned out, albeit in armour that had seen better days. Beside her, the Countess began to climb the stairs, which seemed to make the mandolin-playing guard almost frantic, while the other could only stand and stare. Behind Cloudier, the volume was beginning to grow again.

'Countess?' said the Countess, in a firm but polite tone of voice. 'How do you know I am a countess? I've never been here before.'

The first guard stepped out of the way, mesmerised, as the Countess moved past him. Cloudier saw the mandolineer set his eyes in a distant stare once again.

'Ermm. Just heard you were coming, Countess,' he said, but even he didn't sound convinced.

Behind Cloudier, a stern-looking woman piped up.

'Come along, woman!' she called. 'Order of precedence! If anyone is to gain access, I, as both a duchess and an abbess, should . . .' But she chuntered into silence as the Countess turned a look of polite enquiry her way.

'Sir,' she said, turning back to the guard, who was now so nervous that he had stopped playing his mandolin. 'I believe we can help. If you allow us access to His Grace, and find someone to provide warm drinks for the good people here and outside, I am sure we can find a solution to the Count's predicament.'

'No!' said the guard vehemently. 'Nothing can be done. Nothing! It's gone too far!'

Finally Cloudier clicked. She tugged the Countess's dress, and whispered in her proffered ear.

'Is this him?'

'Yes,' whispered the Countess. And then, turning to the guard once more, so quietly only the three of them would hear: 'Cloudier, meet His Grace Heinz-Marie Von fforbes-Martinez, the Count of Eisberg.'

'Pleased to meet you, Cloudier,' said the Count from

36

under his tin helmet, a look of pale relief crossing his face. 'Sorry about the cannon. I didn't expect people to turn up!'

In a wood-panelled room, a face cracked in a smile. It was a much older, much more experienced smile than had been there a few minutes before. Tiny wrinkles round the eyes spoke of years of such smiles, and the wobbly jowls below seemed to be purpose built for jollity. Even the eyes, often said to be the windows to the soul, seemed to be those of a kindly gent, with a joke for every occasion and a pocket full of humbugs.

Despite what people say – even eyes can lie.

'*I* will find it *first*,' said the face. '*I* will find it. *I. I*, Captain.'

The smile faded, and its owner turned away. Leaving his previous life in a pile by the mirror, he opened a door and stepped out of the wood-panelled room.

'And so you see, the cat had fallen clean out of the bucket!' laughed the Countess, finishing off one of her favourite ice-breaking anecdotes. The Count laughed despite himself, and even Cloudier cracked a grin. It was a great anecdote.

They were now a little further into the castle, in a slightly more comfortable but barely less dilapidated room. There was a trestle table against the wall, with a paltry array of sausage rolls and a mucky punchbowl on it. Three sad little balloons bobbed against the ceiling above. The Count was sitting on a hard wooden chair, having given the only upholstered seat available to the Countess. They were drinking tea, which the Count had made himself, and the Countess was talking, charmingly and wittily, about life on the Galloon. Cloudier felt that the meeting had the atmosphere of an informal afternoon tea party, if it weren't for the hubbub of plummy voices just beyond the door.

The Count was listening very intently, as people tended to do when the Countess spoke, but every once in a while he twitched or blinked as a raised voice from outside the room impinged on their conversation.

'So . . .' the Countess said, as a particularly violent twitch caused the Count to drop his biscuit. 'We've come a long way. The Bilgepump Orchestra has been rehearsing specially for you. Let's talk about your party.'

The Count stared into the middle distance for a short while, and then the floodgates opened.

'I thought it was the right thing to do, and usually I send out hundreds of invitations and get perhaps twenty replies, which is fine because we can use the snug, but this time I sent out hundreds of invitations and got thousands of replies, because I may have mentioned, just in passing, that the Captain and his

Galloon might be part of the celebrations, and everybody has heard about his bride and wants to ask him about it and now I haven't got enough room to have a party that big because the roof has fallen in over the great hall and I can't afford to fix it and it's just me and Hawthorne the guard and my valet, Pill, but I can't find Pill anywhere and I think he's left me because of all this fuss and last night I had to do my own toothbrush and it didn't even go foamy and I asked Hawthorne why that would be and he laughed at me and said, "Have you never heard of toothpaste?", and I said no because someone's always done it for me and how . . . how . . .' A long sob racked his body as snot dripped off his nose and into his tea.

He took a deep breath, as if he were sucking up all the sadness in the world, before finishing: 'And how can I have a party for thousands of posh rich people when they all think I'm posh and rich as well but I'm not rich at all and my valet has left me and I don't even know about tooooooothpaaaaaste!!?'

He clattered his teacup onto the tray, wiped his nose with the back of his sleeve, and threw his arms theatrically around the Countess of Hammerstein's neck. She put her arms round him, and Cloudier watched as her eyes took on the familiar look of a woman making a plan.

After a couple of 'there, there's', the Countess

39

placed the Count's arms back on his lap and stood up carefully. She beckoned Cloudier to follow her, and walked towards the door they had come in by. Cloudier watched as she opened the door, and whispered something to the guard Hawthorne, who they now knew to be the only remaining member of staff in the whole castle. Hawthorne stepped aside, and the Countess walked out onto the top of the flight of steps. The hubbub in the room, which had only been growing in volume, suddenly died down.

The Countess carried on walking down the steps, somehow getting through the crowd without having to push, and exited through the door to the courtyard. Cloudier followed and the crowd, without needing to be told, followed too, in a long and almost orderly line. Cloudier heard a few straggling voices saying things like, 'True class, you know. Her father was a great man,' before being hushed, as the crowd gathered once again outside, where the drivers were waiting in the cold. The Countess stepped onto the running board of a fine old carriage and cleared her throat. Everyone in the crowd leaned forward slightly. She smiled, and everyone leaned forward slightly further.

A rotund lady in a heavy crinoline dress leaned a little too far in her eagerness to hear, and pitched forward onto her face.

'She's gone again!' called her husband, laughing despite himself.

'Don't mind me, I shall have a snooze while I'm down here!' called the fallen lady, from underneath a flouncy bonnet. Silence descended again.

'My Lords, Ladies and gentlemen,' said the Countess. 'The Count of Eisberg and I would like to apologise for keeping you waiting. We just had a few last-minute details to discuss, before being able to reveal to you our little secret. Do forgive us our whims. The Grand Winter Ball is not, after all, to be held here at Castle Eisberg, the Count's ancestral home.'

The crowd began to murmur, with either disappointment or excitement, Cloudier was not sure which. Silence descended again as the Countess raised a hand. A contented snore rose from the pile of crinoline – everyone else was rapt.

'We will instead, be holding it in a place loaned to the Count by one of his oldest and most trusted friends. I would like to invite you all to follow me to the grand ballroom on the Great Galloon of Captain Meredith Anstruther!'

The place erupted – everyone from General Lord Balcony Justice, the fourth Baron Mountebank, down to Little Ern the horse-muck boy, cheered and threw their hats in the air. The Countess was beaming and waving, and gesturing towards the sky, though the Galloon could not be seen through the fog.

Cloudier sidled up to her and tapped her on the shoulder.

'Erm . . . Your Grace?' she asked surreptitiously. 'Do you think the Captain will be okay with this?'

Still smiling, the Countess spoke through perfect pearly teeth.

'I hope so, Cloudier,' she said. 'I really do.'

A short while later, Stanley was staggering through the mess kitchen with a huge pile of silver plates in his arms. They were hot from the washing-up water, and they teetered alarmingly as he staggered about.

'Onto the trolley, Stanley!' called Cook, a big bristly man with the look about him of a portly pirate.

'I'm trying!' called Stanley, as the pile threatened to escape from him.

'Then back here for a bucket of cutlery!' called Cook, who was always quite brusque, but who now had a slight air of panic. 'One thousand, one hundred people all in all, and each expecting a feast! I shall need all the help I can get!'

'Yes!' said Stanley as he crashed the plates onto a waiting trolley, to be taken along to the ballroom. 'If Rasmussen were here, she could . . .'

'One young girl will not be enough!' said Cook. 'We need an army of people. It's not just the setting and decorations, there's a buffet to be made and laid, drinks to prepare, and heaven knows what else. Wonderful as she is, the Countess has gone too far this time! It can't be done . . . can't be done . . .'

It occurred to Stanley, not for the first time, that while complaining about not being able to do something, the cook was simultaneously doing it. With his small staff of helpers, he was rushing about his little kitchen, piling plates, chopping veg, rolling pastry, counting spoons, and generally making ready for a ball. The message had reached the Galloon a short while before, by virtue of the Count's firework-messaging system. The Grand Winter Ball was coming aboard. 1,100 people, with very high expectations, would expect to be fed, watered, entertained and impressed.

Cook dropped another pile of plates into his arms, and almost yelled at him to take them up to the ball-room, and to report back on proceedings up there. So Stanley plonked them on the now-full trolley, and stepping on the tread board at the back, pushed off and

43

along the corridor, with the panicky sounds of the kitchen dying away behind him. He entered a kind of wooden elevator, and pulled a lever. The doors began to close, but were stopped by a young man in a stripy jumper and a woolly hat.

'Sorry, Stanley!' said Clamdigger, one of the Galloon's busiest people. 'Got to get onboard – busy work with the boatswain's chair coming up!'

The door closed, and the lift began to move upwards.

'Have you heard of the Chimney Isles?' asked Stanley, knowing that Clamdigger was almost as good as he was at being outside the right door at the right time, and so may well have heard something.

'Yes – everyone has, haven't they?' said Clamdigger, surprised.

'No,' said Stanley. 'Not me.'

'Pff!' laughed Clamdigger, though not unkindly. 'What do they teach you at school?'

'Nothing,' said Stanley. 'I don't go to school. But that's beside the point. What does everyone know about the Chimney Isles?'

'The Chimney Isles,' said Clamdigger, his voice lowering dramatically, 'are a mysterious chain of islands, peppered with active volcanoes and dramatic lakes of lava. It is perilous to set foot there for all sorts of reasons. Huge eruptions are common, as are rivers of magma and boiling geysers. They are part of the Countship of Eisberg, but no one lives there. Too dangerous.'

'Corks,' said Stanley, as the lift lurched to a stop. 'Why would the Captain be interested in them?'

'The Galloon has been there!' said Clamdigger excitedly, as he and Stanley manoeuvred the trolley out of the lift. 'We circled around the Isles a year or two ago, but the Count chased us off.'

'Why?' said Stanley, utterly intrigued but also concentrating on getting his trolley to go straight.

'Not sure – some private errand of the Captain's,' said Clamdigger. 'I better rush – there's a thousand or so people to bring onboard. But I'll keep an ear out. Could be an adventure in the offing, if we're heading to the Chimney Isles!'

With which he ran off ahead, along the corridor towards the main deck, while Stanley veered off towards the ballroom.

An adventure! thought Stanley. *Crikey. I don't know what's taking Rasmussen so long. 'Getting ready' indeed. She'll be cross if she misses this . . .*

The firework message still hung in the air as Cloudier piloted her weather balloon alongside the Galloon once more.

Great news! Ball going ahead – onboard Galloon.
Please prepare for imminent arrival of 1,100 party-
goers. Thank you, darlings. Hammerstein.

With Cloudier in the tiny craft, were the Countess
herself, the Count of Eisberg, and Hawthorne, the
guard. Cloudier could tell that Hawthorne was fiercely
loyal to the Count, and was pleased that the Count
had such a stalwart friend. Hawthorne leaned out of
the balloon as they approached the edge of the Galloon,
and heaved out one of the sandbags as a buffer. They
bumped slightly as the two craft, one tiny, one huge,
met, and then the Countess was whistling in her demure
yet ear-splitting way, to a crewman on deck.

'Coming aboard, Master Trump!' she called. 'Myself
and one thousand, one hundred and three friends!'

'Aye, miss!' called Trump, breath steaming as
he approached the rail. 'Preparations afoot, as you
requested!'

The portly skysailor gestured behind him, and
Cloudier looked out across the deck of the gigantic
ship. As far as the eye could see, people were busying
themselves, erecting canopies and braziers, sweeping,
clearing away ropes and chests, and generally making
ready for an influx of people. As usual, she was
impressed but not surprised by the quiet efficiency with
which the Gallooniers went about such preparations.

She resolved to write a paean to them as soon as she had time to look up what one was, but in the meantime there was the matter of the approaching aristocrats, their servants and helpers.

'Very good, Trump, very good indeed. Thank you so much,' said the Countess, as she was helped over the rail and onto the deck via a small set of steps. 'This is the Count of Eisberg, whom I would very much like to take to see the Captain, if at all possible – do we know where he might be?'

'Yes'm,' said Trump. 'Map room, ma'am, a-plotting of routes and so forth.'

'Of course,' said the Countess, and it seemed to Cloudier that this had saddened her slightly. 'Why would a little thing like this stop him from a-plotting of routes, and so forth? Very well, we will meet him in his lair.'

With that, the Countess took the hand of the Count of Eisberg, as he stepped over the rail. Once he was safely aboard she thanked Cloudier for all her help, shook Hawthorne's hand, and led Eisberg away, muttering, 'Of course he'll want to see you, Heinz. I'm sure he doesn't hold a grudge . . .'

'Come on,' said Cloudier to Hawthorne, once they had left. 'I'll take you to see Cook – best cup of tea in the seven skies. Then we can go and help with the . . .'

But she tailed off. There was Clamdigger, winding the winch on the boatswain's chair as fast as his long arms would let him, with Able Skyman Abel standing by, looking officious and pumped up as ever in his fur hat and leather gloves.

'. . . crowned heads of the world, here, onboard the Galloon! A mighty honour indeed, young Jack, and you'd do well to remember it. Not the usual shower, pleasant enough though they are, in their earthy way.'

Clamdigger managed a weary raise of the eyebrows as Cloudier walked past, followed by the guard.

'Preparations?' said Hawthorne, guessing the end of the sentence that Cloudier had left hanging.

'Every second Thursday, give or take,' said Cloudier distractedly.

'Sorry, miss?'

'Um? Oh,' Cloudier realised she had been talking nonsense, and shook her head in embarrassment. 'Sorry – yes. Help with the preparations. Mr Trump, I wonder if you could . . .?'

'Of course, Miss Peele,' said the crewman. 'I'll show Mr – Hawthorne, was it? – to the mess. Anything else I can help you with?'

'Yes, pleasantly so, for the time of year,' said Cloudier, staring at Clamdigger once again.

'So, Miss Peele,' said Skyman Abel, once the two men had moved off. 'I expect it was magnificent, eh?

All those fine people, the crème de la crème, all in one place! And to think they're coming here! Keep winding, my lad, no slacking. It's going to take all day to bring all the guests up one by one!'

'Well, Mr Abel, we've brought the Galloon as low as she can safely go over the castle, so it won't take as long as all that but still . . . perhaps we could take it in turns?' said Clamdigger, although he showed no sign of being out of puff.

'Tish and pish, boy! I'm the welcoming attaché!'

'Bless you' said Cloudier mischievously, making Clamdigger chuckle.

'I can't be seen doing manual labour when the nobility and gentry of half the world arrives onboard! No, if I'm to make the most of this opportunity, I need to be seen to be above such things. So keep winding, there's eleven hundred or so to go!

With this he peered over the edge as if hoping to see 1,100 members of the aristocracy peering back up at him, despite the fog.

'Are there really that many people coming onboard?' Clamdigger asked Cloudier while Abel's back was turned.

'Yes, but they're not all posh – at least half of them are the drivers, ladies' maids and whatnot,' she said. 'Also, I think it's safe to say they won't all be needing the boatswain's chair.'

49

'Why's that?' asked Clamdigger.

'Look!' said Cloudier, pointing out across the sky, to where strange shapes were just beginning to emerge from the mist.

Clamdigger looked, and they heard a squeak from Abel, as the shapes began to manifest themselves. Coming out of the clouds, only a few tens of metres from the Galloon, was an array of vehicles such as Cloudier had never seen. The first was a kind of charabanc, an open-topped omnibus, with a bamboo propeller at the front and two canvas wings stretching out alongside, grey smoke puffing from a chimney in the bonnet.

Next to that was a gyrocopter, pedal-powered by a bowler-hatted man, with two maids and a duke hanging grimly onto its spindly frame. Behind that were four or five more contraptions, including a small biplane, a thing that looked like a papier-mâché space rocket, and even a balloon, although this one had apparently been popped, as it squirted erratically about the sky, trailing a gondola-shaped basket chock-full of nobles and real people. Cloudier saw that the basket was actually a modified wagon, and it still had the horse attached, dangling stoically from the harness like a huge, misshapen fluffy dice. The caval-cade of aircraft had reached them, and as the first vehicle flew overhead, she heard a cheer from the

Gallooniers, and a kind of jolly braying from the charabanc full of aristocrats.

'Fine day for it, miss!' called Charlie, from the driving seat, waving at Cloudier as he passed a few feet overhead, between the deck and the array of balloons and sails that kept the Galloon in the air.

'Glad to see you made it!' cried Cloudier, much to Skyman Abel's annoyance.

'Wouldn't miss it for the world, no I wouldn't!' he called back, as he brought the charabanc, chugging and coughing, down onto the deck.

'Miss Peele!' said Skyman Abel sharply. 'May I remind you that the focus of our attentions must be the ball guests, not the help, who can . . .'

'Charlie is a ball guest!' interrupted Cloudier, shooting an embarrassed look at the chauffeur, who waved his hand dismissively at Abel.

'I think not!' spluttered Abel.

'Ermm . . .' said Clamdigger, still heaving on the chair-winch.

'This is the birthday celebration of his Grace the Count Heinz-Marie Von fforbes-Martinez of Eisberg! Attended by the great and the good! I doubt that Charlie the wagon driver is on the guest list!' said Abel, looking around for someone to share his joke with, but finding no one.

'I think the Captain . . .' began Cloudier.

'I think the Captain understands the situation and will provide the lower orders with refreshments befitting their situation in the mess or . . . or . . .' said Abel, but his sentence faded as Clamdigger grabbed him by the arm and turned him round.

'Ermm . . .' said the cabin boy. 'Let's find out what he thinks.'

And with that he pointed up towards the quarterdeck, where the Captain habitually stood when making pronouncements or giving what amounted to orders, although he would always have denied giving any such thing. There he stood, somehow lit from behind, despite the fog. And he spake thusly:

'People of the Great Galloon – please make welcome our friends from all over the north and beyond, who are here for a party. The preparations are almost finished, in record time even for us, and the ballroom awaits. The guest of honour is of course my old and very dear friend the Count of Eisberg. I am pleased to announce that our recent feud is in a state of truce for the evening.' A ragged cheer went up. 'I would also like to make it clear that the invitation extends to *all* of our guests equally.'

Cloudier thought she saw the Captain's head turn towards Abel at this point, but he was a long way off so it was hard to tell. Another cheer went up at his words although Cloudier saw more than a little sniffing and eye rolling.

'Everybody will of course be expected to pitch in with washing-up, serving drinks and so on, but I know a good time will be had by all. The ball is officially open. Enjoy.'

This caused a bit of a furore amongst the snootier guests, but in general there was a feeling of joyous expectation as people made their way towards the hatches that led below.

As the last of the flying contraptions landed amongst the crates and nets on deck, Cloudier saw Charlie bringing the charabanc round to take off again. 'Just off to collect more guests – we'll have them up here before you can say, "Happy birthday, Count Heinz-Marie von fforbes-Martinez of Eisberg"!' he called, as the charabanc lifted off.

Clamdigger, now helping a cheerful older lady out of the boatswain's chair, smiled and waved along with Cloudier, but Abel had a face like thunder.

'Washing-up? Serving drinks? Hell in a handcart, I tell you!' he grumbled as he wandered off, without even saying hello to the new arrival.

Cloudier and Clamdigger laughed, and to their delight the new arrival did too.

'Well,' she said. 'He seems a little stuck up, if I may say so. And I may, because I'm a marquess and I can say what I like!'

*　　*　　*

'Her Imperial Highness the Sultana of Magrabor, Harness of the Four Winds, Empress of the Lowest Lands, May She Reign Forever if She Wishes. Known as Doris. With her the Infanta Marguerite and His Grace the Count of Three.'

This was the voice of Snivens, standing in the doorway of the grand ballroom, announcing guests as they entered. Stanley was impressed that he seemed to know everybody without referring to the list which the Countess had pressed into his hand. Another group approached.

'The Duc d'Orange, Hattie the stable girl, Princess Chartreau of Youlouse, and Footman Turtle,' called Snivens. He didn't quite have the Captain's trick of making himself heard above the background noise, so his voice already sounded a little strained.

Stanley watched the small group go by, then stepped up to Snivens before the next group made themselves known.

'Hello, Snivens!' he said. 'Have you seen . . .'

'Betty Philpott of Lower Mile, King Parentheses the Nineteenth, and Keith,' said Snivens.

'Yes, but what about . . .' said Stanley.

'Huggins, Marley Jones, the Marquis of Daub, and Little Ern,' said Snivens.

'Very nice too, but what about . . .' said Stanley.

'One moment, Stanley,' said the butler. 'Wiggo the

Drive, Captain Westerly-Breeze, and the Lady Marianna of Hammerstein.'

Stanley had stepped out of the way of the guests, and was now standing behind Snivens. He whispered in his ear.

'Please, Mr Snivens, if you have any idea where Rasmussen is, I'm beginning to worry about her,' he hissed.

'The Lady Marianna of Hammerstein,' repeated Snivens.

Stanley glanced at the shiny pink puffball of a girl in front of him.

'Yes, hello,' he said, then turned back to Snivens' ear. 'Rasmussen? You know? Small girl, grubby? Often rude?'

'Not grubby now,' said the Lady Marianna of Hammerstein, poking Stanley in the bum with a parasol she didn't need because they were indoors. 'Still happy to be rude though, when it's necessary.'

Stanley spun towards the girl, and only as he looked at her face did he realise what a fool he'd been. Rasmussen was the daughter of the Countess, he knew that. And her first name was Marianna, he knew that. But he had never thought of her as posh before. Yet here she was, dressed in a kind of satin globe, adorned with lace and ribbons and rosettes and veils and a big gold necklace and a bustle and a parasol, so that the

55

only bit of Rasmussen still visible was her shiny cheeks, almost as pink as her dress.

He looked at her in disbelief, as she opened a largish compact with a kitten's face on it, that hung on a chain round her neck. She took out a sponge, and soon a cloud of pink powder surrounded her, which she then blew towards Stanley and Snivens, covering them both in rose-scented talc.

'Corks and blimey,' said Stanley through the cloud.

'It's "corks and blimey, *ma'am*", if you don't mind, young man!' said Rasmussen, deadpan. And then they both bent double with laughter.

'Think of the trouble we can cause with you looking like that!' gasped Stanley through his tears.

Cloudier stood quietly in the corner of the Captain's map room, unsure of the reason for her summoning. The Captain had just returned from giving his welcome speech, and now the two men were sitting at the table, eating grilled cheese with their boots off.

'It's a terrible thing, this business with your brother, a terrible thing indeed,' said the Count, as he took a sip of the Captain's finest port wine.

'Aye, Heinz, a terrible thing it is. And I'm glad you see it that way. I thought you might still be sore.'

'Sore?' said the Count, genuinely confused. 'My word, no. I never was. Sneaking around the Chimney

Isles without permission – well that was just plain rude, and I had to chase you away. But for marrying Isabella? Not a bit of it. Neither of us wanted it, in truth. There's no true marriage where there's no true love.'

'So it's true, I assume? The truce?' said the Captain.

'It is, and not just for this evening. I am grateful to you for allowing my people and me onboard.'

'Would you like to sit, Ms Peele?' rumbled the Captain, making Cloudier's pulse race.

'No, thank you, sir. Thank you,' she said. 'Just here because you asked me to come down, very pleased, though. Thank you.'

'Of course,' said the Captain. 'We won't keep you long. My discussion with the Count here affects you too.'

Cloudier's mind was a whirl, as she tried to think what she could possibly have to do with this situation.

'Lookout,' said the Captain.

Cloudier ducked.

'No,' he continued with a half-smile. 'You are a very fine lookout. Your work in the affair of the flying monster moths was invaluable.'

'Th'k you, sir,' mumbled Cloudier, unsure where to put her face.

'And we're entering a dangerous phase once more,' said the Captain, kindly ignoring her terror.

'Are we?' asked the Count, twisting in his chair to keep Cloudier in his eye line. 'But we're here in Eisberg, my home. What danger could we possibly be in?'

'I must start once again by making it absolutely clear that this is my quest, and I do not expect you to follow me,' said the Captain quietly. 'If you do follow me, and choose to help me, I will do everything in my power to keep you safe. Do you understand?'

'Of course, Meredith . . .' began the Count, but he was quickly shushed.

'I speak to Cloudier,' said the Captain. 'Your help will be appreciated, but your decisions are your own.'

'Oh,' said Cloudier. 'Of course, I'll help however I can.'

'It will mean missing the ball,' said the Captain gravely.

'Oh pur-lease!' snorted Cloudier. 'Who wants to go to the snotty old ball any . . . way . . .'

She faded out as the Count's face took on a crestfallen expression.

'Errr, though it will be the party of the century, clearly . . .' she finished lamely.

'Cloudier is something of a wallflower,' explained the Captain.

'Hmmm,' said the Count, looking at the floor.

'I would like you to take to the skies once more, in your weather balloon. Keep an eye out for the Grand Sumbaroon of Zebediah Anstruther, who will, I believe, be here before long.'

'Yes, sir, of course.' Cloudier loved being in her weather balloon. It gave her a chance to read, and to write, and to cultivate an image of being distant and interesting.

'It will not be a jolly,' said the Captain. 'It is imperative that we see the Sumbaroon before he sees us. You will need to use your recently gained expertise in piloting the weather balloon away from the Galloon.'

He slammed his finger down on a map, and fixed Cloudier with a firm but kindly gaze.

'Head for the Chimney Isles,' he said.

'No!' cried out the Count. 'It's too dangerous. I won't allow it! The Chimney Isles are in my lands. Besides, she's just a girl!'

'You will allow it, or you will find yourself holding your ball down in Castle Eisberg. And Cloudier will decide what is and isn't possible.'

'But why, Meredith?' said the Count. 'What interest could Zebediah possibly have in the Chimney Isles?'

The Captain was now staring at his coffee mug, not making eye contact with either of them.

'There is a token,' he said, almost inaudibly. 'Or rather half a token. Made of gold mined from the Chimney Isles. In form it is like a large coin or a medal, with a picture of the Galloon on one side, and a series of symbols and glyphs on the other. I had it dug from the earth, I had it made, and I had it broken in two.

60

The last time I was here, Heinz, when you chased me off. Half of it I gave to Isabella. It is a token of our love.'

'So with your half of the token, we can prove that you are indeed Meredith, not Zebediah!' cried Cloudier, then sat back, embarrassed. The Captain did not look up.

'Yes,' he said. 'And more. It is vital to the future of the Galloon itself. I have a suspicion that Zebediah has heard about this token, and seeks it.'

'So he'll come here? Right?' said the Count, caught up despite himself.

'Yes, he'll never get it from you, will he? You can prove that you're the rightful captain, and Isabella will be yours again! We only have to wait!' said Cloudier excitedly.

'Yes, that would be the case . . . if I hadn't . . . if I hadn't . . .' said the Captain, chewing his lip.

'Yes?' said Cloudier.

'Yes?' said the Count.

'If I hadn't dropped it down a volcano by accident,' said the Captain sheepishly.

'Ah!' said the Count and Cloudier together.

'Pleased to meet you I'm sure, Your Magnificence', said Rasmussen to a large man in a kaftan. 'What a lovely fabric your dress is made of. And how lucky you were to find so much of it!'

61

The man goggled, unsure whether he had been insulted or not, as Rasmussen moved on, with Stanley chuckling in her wake.

'This is Lady O'Grady, and her new husband, Fondly,' said the Countess as they approached another group.

'Charmed, I'm sure,' said Rasmussen with a little curtsey. 'Tell me, Mr Fondly, what first attracted you to the famously wealthy and frail Lady O'Grady?'

Lady O'Grady coughed, as if to prove her frailty, while Fondly puffed himself up like a vol-au-vent.

'My daughter, the Lady Marianna of Hammerstein,' said the Countess quickly, stifling a smile.

'Ah,' said Fondly awkwardly. 'Pleased to meet you, I'm sure, My Lady.'

'The pleasure is all yours,' said Rasmussen, with a smile so sickly it even smelled of treacle.

'My Lady!' muttered Stanley, laughing behind his hand as he stood beside Rasmussen.

'Yes?' said Lady O'Grady to Stanley, with a sharp look.

'No,' said Stanley, 'I was just laughing at Rasmussen being called "My Lady". I've never . . .'

'It's funny, is it, for a person of rank to be addressed correctly?' snapped O'Grady.

'Person of . . ..?' said Stanley, confused.

'I'm sure Stanley . . .' began the Countess, but Lady O'Grady's dander was up.

'I am grateful to the Captain for allowing the ball to proceed, but his insistence on this . . . this . . . *integration* . . . between nobility and the common sort . . .'

'Common sort yourself!' said Rasmussen, glowering now from beneath her assortment of tiaras and bows.

'Really!' said O'Grady, glaring at Stanley as if it had been he who spoke. 'If young people cannot comport themselves politely, perhaps they should be asked to leave . . .'

She stuttered to a halt as it became clear to her that everyone was looking at the Countess for guidance on what to do next.

'Yes,' said the Countess quietly. 'In the Captain's absence, attendance at the ball is at Snivens' discretion. I must make it clear right now that rude and unwelcoming behaviour cannot be tolerated.'

Lady O'Grady clasped her hands in front of her bosom, and stared triumphantly at Stanley, but he couldn't help noticing that the Countess had been addressing her remarks at Lady O'Grady herself. He took a breath to say as much, when behind him he heard Snivens announce yet more guests to the ball, which was already thrumming with activity.

'His Grace the Earl O'Dawes, along with his son Paddy. Baron Farquhar, Margery Gusset and . . . erm . . .' said the butler.

Stanley and Rasmussen turned to look. No one else

seemed to notice anything amiss. The Bilgepump Orchestra struck up a jolly reel, and chatter continued about them as the newcomers joined the throng. But for Snivens to miss a name seemed strange to Stanley. Not only did he have a prodigious memory and an encyclopaedic knowledge, he had the list of guests that the Countess had provided. As Stanley watched, Snivens took the list out of his pocket and fluttered through it, while apologising to the newcomer.

'Odd,' said Rasmussen, next to Stanley.

'Yes,' said Stanley. 'Who is that man?'

'No idea. Mum?' she turned to the Countess, who had been back in conversation with the group. The Countess turned to look.

'Hmm,' she said. 'Not sure. Seems vaguely familiar though. Perhaps he was a last-minute replacement for someone?'

And she turned back to the grown-ups' conversation, which was currently about the price of hay.

The man on the steps was now standing close to Snivens, looking over his shoulder at the list. He was a smooth-faced, jowly man, with a smile that somehow seemed more sad than happy. Stanley put this down to embarrassment at being left off the list. He moved closer, to try and hear what was being said.

'Tell me what they say,' said Rasmussen as he left. 'I'll try and find out who knows him.'

'Roger Willco,' said Stanley.

'Is he?' said Rasmussen.

'Is he what?' said Stanley.

'Is that him? Roger Willco?'

'No. Roger Willco means "I understand what you've said, and will do as you ask",' said Stanley.

'Oh. It's a very confusing and silly way of saying a simple thing. Please speak more clearly in future,' said Rasmussen, clucking like a hen.

'Right. Yes. Roger Wil . . . I mean, I understand and will do as you ask,' said Stanley, abashed.

'Very good,' said Rasmussen.

Stanley, thinking that perhaps this little madam act was getting to Rasmussen a bit too much, moved closer to the steps where Snivens now stood, listening to the newcomer, who was whispering in his ear.

'Erm!' said Snivens aloud, once the man had finished speaking. 'Mr Fassbinder, special aide to erm . . . somebody . . .'

At this point Mr Fassbinder seemed to find someone in the crowd whom he knew, and with a little wave he dived into the throng. Stanley approached Snivens conspiratorially.

'All well, Mr Snivens?' he asked, watching Mr Fassbinder chatting to a couple of lords and a chambermaid.

'Ah . . . yes, I'm sure . . .' said Snivens distractedly.

'It's just . . . I didn't quite catch who he said he was with, and he's not on the list. But he seemed a nice enough chap . . .'

'Curiouser and curiouser,' said Stanley.

'You mean "curious and more curious",' said Snivens, ever the stickler.

'Yes,' said Stanley. 'I suppose I do.'

And so once more Cloudier was preparing to go up in her weather balloon. She stood by the iron ring that attached it to the deck near the stern of the Galloon, while Tarheel and Clamdigger winched it in.

'So you're chief lookout now?' said Clamdigger as he heaved.

'No, just, you know, helping out, I suppose,' said Cloudier, wary of seeming to be too much of a captain's pet.

'Maybe I could come up to the weather balloon at some point and help?' said Clamdigger.

Tarheel's good eye glittered with mischief.

'Erm,' said Cloudier, embarrassed. 'Don't you usually keep lookout from the crow's nest?'

'Yes, but . . .' stuttered Clamdigger.

'I mean, not that . . .' stammered Cloudier.

'Here we are, young miss,' said Tarheel, pulling the balloon's little basket over at an angle so that Cloudier could climb in.

'Thanks,' she said. 'I suppose you could . . .'

'Erm, no. You're right. Should get to the crow's nest really,' said Clamdigger, and he began to let the rope out from its winch.

'Maybe I'll write you a poem,' said Cloudier inexplicably.

'That'd be nice, miss,' said Tarheel.

'No, I mean, oh, never mind,' said Cloudier, raising her voice as the weather balloon picked up speed.

'If you like!' called Clamdigger. Cloudier was not sure whether his tone was resigned or pleased, and he was now receding as the balloon pulled further and further away from the Galloon, though it was still connected by its sturdy rope.

'I do like!' she called lamely, just as the first of the many sails and balloons came between them. She thought she heard Tarheel's throaty laugh, which didn't make her feel any better. Still, she thought, at least with all this miscommunication she had something to feel sorry for herself about, and therefore something to put into verse.

They were still moored up to Castle Eisberg, and the Captain had asked her to stay put for a short while, until he had made plans for her, so she should have a little while to get on with some poetry before the work task started in earnest.

Only it wasn't as easy as that. With an understanding

that poetry wasn't just self-pity that rhymed, had come the realisation that she wasn't very good at it. She had read and re-read her small volume of verse, and had learned much, but writing her own verse had become harder, not easier. However, she was determined to try, and her apparent inability to communicate with her best friend Clamdigger was as good a place as any to start.

She opened her trusty notebook and took out a pen.

Shall I Compare Thee To A . . . she began to write. No, too obvious.

How Do I Quite Like Thee . . . No, not thee. She'd been that way before. How about something more freeform in style?

Clamdigger.
    Stripy long figure.
Talking,
  but not quite
Saying
  Anything.
Many things.
    Left
      Unsaid.
Left in his head.
    Like bread.
     In a breadbin.

'Hmm,' she allowed. 'It's a new direction, I suppose.'

'KKWWAAAARRRKK!' said a voice beside her, making her throw her pen overboard and slam her book shut on her fingers.

'SQUEEEEEE – HAK – HAK – HAK – HAK – KWAARRRRRRRKKK!' screamed the nightmarish figure now sitting on the rim of the basket, staring directly into her soul with red eyes like hot coals.

'Oh my word!' squeaked Cloudier from behind a cushion, aware that this perhaps wasn't the image of insouciance she normally tried to project. She was relieved to see that she knew the owner of this voice, though this was only the second time they had met.

'Errr, hello, Fishbane,' she managed, as she righted herself and made an attempt to smooth down her hair.

'SKKWWAAAAAAAKKKK-EEK-EEK-EEK-EEEEEEEEEK-AAARRRRKKKKK!' said Fishbane politely, then he dropped from sight behind the edge of the basket.

Fishbane was a Seagle, a kind of enormous seabird, with a razor-sharp beak and talons like dragon's teeth, but surprisingly helpful once you got to know him. He had helped Cloudier before, and she knew him to be a friend of the Captain's from some previous adventure.

'FKWARK!' he opined, as he popped up again with Cloudier's pen in his beak.

Cloudier knew him well enough to know what he wanted. She held her notebook up to him, and he looked at it with what seemed to her like murderous hatred. But, with the pen sticking out of his beak, he began to write. Cloudier had seen this before, but it was no less fascinating for that. When he had finished, he winked, and dropped again from sight, making hideous squawking noises as he went.

Cloudier gingerly turned the notebook round, to see what Fishbane had written. She was not surprised to see a fluid, cultured hand covering the page.

This is what it said:

Greetings, purple-feathered verse-striver, from Fishbane, lord of three of the four winds.

Cloudier was pleased to see that the letter was addressed to her this time, rather than the Captain, though she wasn't sure how she felt about being addressed as 'purple-feathered verse-striver'. She read on.

Pleased am I that the good Captain heeded my words, and has the Chimney Isles in his sights. But he must hurry. Zebediah, curse the very name, is closer than he thinks, and has some mischief afoot. Word amongst the weed-people is that the Sumbaroon has spies abroad. A bitter Pill must be crushed. Look to the working sort. Send warning, rhyme-writer, poet-spy. Yet strike out – the seed that falls far from the tree has more light to grow by.

Fishbane the Wanderer

P.S. Be not afraid of writing 'good' or 'bad' verse. Write much, read more and worry less.

'Hmm,' said Cloudier, partly in response to the worrying news of Zebediah's spies, and partly at being given poetry-writing advice by someone who would use a phrase like 'the seed that falls far from the tree has more light to grow by'.

Despite his rather pompous style, she knew that Fishbane was right – she should strike out, take the weather balloon off to see what she could see. She took a small brass compass out of her pocket and checked it. She stuck a finger in the air to test the wind speed and direction. She looked about her to get her bearings. The mountains around Eisberg lowered over her in the twilight, and would be difficult to get beyond, but she felt that she could do it, and perhaps she owed it to the Captain, who was stuck here being diplomatic with the Count.

Dramatically, she ripped a page from her notebook,

and then wished she hadn't, as she struggled to write on it. She leaned on the edge of the basket, and scribbled.

Mother,
I'm going off for a while. Please don't try and follow me. There are some things I need to do.
C.

She read it through, and was pleased with its sparseness and sense of mystery. But she couldn't bear to be the cause of worry, so she added a postscript.

P.S. I'm taking the weather balloon to look for the Grand Sumbaroon. The Captain asked me to help, and Fishbane will be looking out for me. I've included his message here. I've got thermal undies, and a packed dinner. Back by morning. Love you, Cloudier.

She folded the two letters together and placed them in one of the rocket-shaped capsules she used to communicate with the Galloon. After winding its clockwork mechanism and setting it off down the rope, she waited a short while, until she thought it must have reached the deck. Then, trying not to think too hard about what she was doing, she untied the balloon and let it fly.

Before long, she was rising quickly past the huge

main balloon of the Galloon which, even though she was hundreds of feet away, filled her entire forward view. Above it, there were a few outrigger sails and a flagpole, and above that a view to the far horizon, with only the Eisberg Mountains and a far distant sea between. Out in that sea were the mountainous Chimney Isles. Cloudier took a deep breath, coughed a little as the cold air hit her throat, and turned round.

'North,' she said decisively.

With only a brief check of her compass, a few misgivings and a little thrill of excitement, she set off into the blue.

On deck, Abel was pacing up and down, worrying. He was out of his depth in front of all the dignitaries down in the ballroom, and he knew it. He desperately wanted to make the most of this opportunity for advancement, to make sure he was firmly in the Captain's good books, but wasn't sure how to go about it.

As he worried and paced, paced and worried, he heard a noise. A kind of fizzing whirr, somewhere above. He looked about and could see nothing except the great balloons and sails way overhead, billowing and bobbing in the wind. All seemed well. Thinking no more of it, he began to pace again.

He had only stepped into the ballroom for a few minutes, and had been simultaneously boggled by the finery on display, and troubled by the preponderance of flat caps and flatter vowels. It didn't seem right to him, this mixing of sorts, drivers and dukes, stable girls and Sultanas, all 'mucking in' together. And yet there must be some way for him to make the most of it, and to make an impression.

'Whirr . . .' went the noise above him. He ignored it.

Perhaps if he could be involved in some kind of derring-do, some attention-grabbing affair that ensured that everyone there would know his name. Something that made the name Able Skyman Abel synonymous with Captain Anstruther.

He stopped pacing and puffed out his chest as the idea began to excite him. He could feel it – this was it. This was the idea that would put his name on the tongues of all the VIPs in the north! He would arrange some kind of escapade in which he was the hero – a robbery he could foil, a fight he could break up, an assassination attempt he could intervene in – and become known as Abel, the Skyman Who Saved The Day!

Standing tall now, his mind whirring with ideas under his big bearskin hat, he began to form a plan. If that lazy boy Clamdigger could be persuaded to . . . no . . . too risky. How about planting something in the Countess's handbag? No, she was too alert . . . something to do with Ms Huntley? She seemed to be ever in the Captain's good books, perhaps it would do her good to be knocked down a peg or two . . .

'Whirr . . .'

'Shhhh!' he hissed unthinkingly. 'I need to think. If only I had reason to accuse someone at the ball of wrongdoing . . .'

'WHIRR . . .'

'Oh, for the love of . . .' he said, and turning round, took the full force of Cloudier's message-rocket, firework and all, square between the eyes.

'Mama . . .' he squeaked, as he fell senseless to the deck.

Beside him, the capsule cracked open, and the letters floated out. The last thing Abel saw was these words:

Sumbaroon has spies abroad . . . look to the working sort . . .

Aha! thought the most devious part of his mind, before blanking out completely.

*   *   *

The ball was now well underway. The Bilgepump Orchestra was playing jigs and reels and polkas and arias, klezmer and bhangra and beats from all over, in an effort to make absolutely everyone feel at home. The ball-goers were having an absolute riot, all previous social awkwardnesses forgotten. Cook was keeping a constant stream of delicious snacks and titbits flowing, and had even managed to come along for a dance or two, while other people stepped into the kitchens. Plates were being cleared away and glasses refreshed by peers of the realm and Peter the goatherd alike, with no one batting an eyelid. Stanley loved every moment of it. He was hurrying to and fro between the dumb waiter and the ballroom, bringing in groaning platters of sausage rolls, plopping them down on a table, and then stopping for a dance or two before hurrying back for more.

'What fun!' brayed a stick-thin woman in glittering pearls, as she was swung off her feet by a small hairy gardener.

'Ey oooopp, Your Maaaaajessty!' growled a pig girl called Grunty, as she bowed low before a bearded king.

'Don't you "Your Majesty" me!' snorted the King, as he took Grunty by the arm and led her towards the bar.

'This is great, isn't it?' Stanley called to Rasmussen,

who was standing on the feet of a footman as they danced.

'Yup!' she called back, and then he heard her telling the footman how the Duchess of Tod had been making eyes at him all evening.

'Really?' said the footman, dropping Rasmussen off his feet as he swept off to find the Duchess.

'She has been making eyes at him!' laughed Rasmussen. 'But only because she wants a biscuit!'

Stanley was confused, until he looked where she was pointing, and saw the footman being introduced to the Duchess of Tod – a large slobbery dog belonging to an old man in a bath chair.

'See?' said Rasmussen. 'People believe what you say when you're wearing fancy pants clothes. You should try it!'

'Hmm. I think it helps if you are also a real-life countess, dripping with jewels and heirlooms,' said Stanley, not unkindly.

'I'm not a countess! My mum is!' Rasmussen snapped, putting away the pendant she had been fiddling with.

'No, sorry. But you will be one day, perhaps,' said Stanley.

'Yes, I suppose these things are all heirlooms – so they will be mine one day.'

Rasmussen seemed to think about this as if it had

never occurred to her before, then she stared fixedly at one spot for a while. Stanley followed her gaze, but couldn't see anything untoward, so he assumed she was just being cross with him.

'Sorry, I didn't mean to be horrible. I like all that . . . pink . . . stuff really. Very regal. So, fancy coming to get some more sausage rolls with me? And maybe a cup of tea?' he said, but she didn't reply, or even look away.

'Look, I said I'm sorry . . .' began Stanley.

'I think we've got some whistle-blowing to do,' said Rasmussen quietly.

'Well, I know it's usually whistle-blowing at four on a Saturday, but . . .' said Stanley, tailing off as he followed Rasmussen's gaze again.

All he saw was a four-square dance going on, on the dance floor. A foursome made up of Charlie the driver, Snivens the Butler, Crewman Tamp and the Sultana of Magrabor was ducking and diving, twisting and swaying in time to instructions shouted from the front by Mr Lungren, leader of the Orchestra. He watched Tamp duck low and move under the arms of the other three, then spin round and stand at his place back in the square, while other dancers in other squares did the same all around him. Then the Sultana did the same; duck, spin and stand. He saw Charlie take his turn; duck, spin, dip and stand. Then Snivens: duck, spin and stand.

'Very nice,' said Stanley. 'Duck, spin and stand. What does that have to do with . . .?'

'Watch again,' said Rasmussen, as the four dancers moved onto other partners. Charlie was still in their line of sight, now standing in formation with Hawthorne, Tarheel and Mr Fassbinder, all tapping their feet as they waited for the musical phrase to begin again.

'Duck, spin and stand,' said Stanley as Hawthorne started the dance.

'Duck, spin and stand,' said Rasmussen, almost under her breath, as Tarheel carried it on.

'Duck, spin, dip and stand,' they said together as Charlie took his turn, and then looked at each other as Mr Fassbinder moved into place.

'*Dip* and stand?' they repeated, and then jumped up from their chairs.

'He's pick-pocketing as he goes!' hissed Rasmussen.

'And it's up to us to stop him!' said Stanley, as they ran towards the dance floor.

Stanley felt the old thrill of excitement. An adventure seemed in the offing once more! He saw Rasmussen dive in between the legs of the many dancers, and followed her unthinkingly. They dodged, trying not to trip anyone as they made a beeline for Charlie.

'And he seemed so nice,' called Stanley as they executed a particularly fancy do-si-do to avoid the tramping feet of an earl.

'You never can tell,' called Rasmussen, and Stanley overtook her. 'Sometimes it's the nice ones you have to look out for.'

They had arrived by Charlie's dancing square, and Stanley wasted no time in leaping at the nefarious driver. He grabbed at Charlie's jacket, and his fingers closed round something. As Charlie spun round in confusion, Stanley yanked his hand away, and with it came a long string of pearls, a slim leather wallet, an assortment of coins, and a medal wrapped in tissue paper. The trinkets flew through the air, and in quick succession Charlie's face registered shock, anger and a kind of hurt innocence.

Tarheel, Hawthorne and the jowly man called Fassbinder stepped back in amazement. Stanley picked up the pearls, and held them aloft. Behind him, Rasmussen cleared her throat and said, in a loud clear voice:

'W—'

And then the doors at the far ended of the ballroom burst open. The music, which had been fading away, stopped completely, and everybody, including Stanley, Rasmussen and Charlie, turned to look.

In through the doors, now thrown back on their hinges, strode Able Skyman Abel, carrying his bearskin hat, and with a bump on his forehead the size of a goose's egg.

'Upladderly, I muscle in on your violence!' he called authoritatively, striding crazily across the floor.

'Eh?' said everyone to each other, or similar noises of confusion.

'Unsnappily, I entrust your connivance!' said Abel again, waving a finger in the air. He stopped briefly, as if realising he was talking drivel.

'What I mean is, "Unhappily, I must insist on your silence!" I'm sorry, I recently chained a crow to my drain!' he explained.

A chorus of 'sorry old chap, no clearer I'm afraid' and similar phrases rose amongst the ball-goers. Abel seemed to realise he was losing his impetus, and shook his head.

'I mean, I'm sorry, I recently sustained a blow to my brain!' he explained again, more clearly this time.

'Aah!' said the assembled throng, please to hear a sentence that actually made sense.

Beside him, Stanley was aware that Charlie was edging away. Before he could tell Rasmussen, Abel spoke again.

'Could the Lords and Ladles – sorry, Ladies – step to one side please? I have reason to believe that one of the "servants" – he almost spat the word, as he leaned desperately on a potted tree for support – 'is a . . . PIE!'

He waited for the reaction this revelation would

cause. It seemed to Stanley that he was disappointed to get a few well-meaning comments like 'Are you quite well, old chap?' and 'Come and have a sit down, mate, you'll feel better'.

Abel looked about himself, confused. Behind Stanley, Rasmussen piped up again.

'Do you mean "spy"?' she asked helpfully.

'Yes!' snapped Abel. 'I do mean spy! A sneaking, conniving impostor, here to do the Captain down! We must unmask him forthwith!'

He was now approaching the throng again, his eyes rolling like a frightened horse as he fought against the concussion that was clearly threatening to send him to sleep.

'No,' said Rasmussen. 'Not a spy. A thief.' And she held up a jewelled brooch that had fallen from Charlie's pocket.

'Oh yeah, a thief!' said a number of voices around Stanley, as people remembered they had been mid-drama when this current drama butted in. Charlie had been sneaking away, but Hawthorne grabbed him firmly by the shoulders. Abel's rant, however, was not over.

'A thief, a spy, a tinker, his wife, her brother, a sailor, poor man, beggar man, three potato four. What does it matter? There is a bad'un on the Galloon, and it is up to me to apprehend him!'

'But we've already . . .' said Stanley.

Before he could finish the thought, though, a number of things happened with shocking speed. Charlie reached out and grabbed a walking stick from an old man nearby. He swished it above his head, clearing a space around him, and then grasped the head of the stick in one hand and the shaft in the other. To Stanley's dismay, he pulled them apart, and Stanley realised that hidden within the stick was a sword, which Charlie now held.

'A sword!' cried a lady in the audience, and pretended to faint, but as nobody caught her, she quietly corrected herself and coughed in embarrassment.

Charlie stood now in a semi-circle of people, open towards Abel, swishing his sword expertly.

'I didn't want no trouble, honest I didn't,' he said, almost convincingly. 'You don't often see this many jewels in a room, and my dear old mum being ill and all . . .'

'Oh, please,' said a gruff-faced man nearby, and then shushed pretty quickly when the sword point appeared by his nose.

'I've rehearsed for moments such as this,' said Charlie sternly. 'So if you'll please let me finish . . .'

'Yes of course,' said the gruff man. 'Sorry, old chap.'

'My creaky old mum is ailing, and only needs a bit of cash for her dear old knees . . . no, sorry . . . it's my mum that's dear, and her knees that are creaky, not the other way round . . . and surely no one will begrudge her that. She has been . . .' he stumbled over his words, and took from his top pocket a crib sheet, which he looked at before continuing. 'She has been a working lady since I was knee high to a ninnyhammer, with nothing to show for it. I take only from those what can afford it . . .'

He was circling now, hoping perhaps to get round Abel and closer to the door, but his luck was not in. Most of the ball-goers were transfixed, and even Stanley was too confused to know what to do for the best, but Abel, in his addled state, had had enough of Charlie's excuses.

'Baldercock and poppydash!' he shouted. 'Or rather, cockerdash and baldypop! You're a thief, no better than you should be, and no doubt your mother was the same.'

A gasp went up from the crowd at this insult, and Charlie's face coloured. He brandished his sword above his head. (Stanley had always wondered what 'brandished' meant, and he was interested to see it done. It meant 'waved about'). Charlie advanced on Abel, who, perhaps because of his recent accident, did not seem quite his usual cowardly self. To Stanley's surprise, he stood his ground as Charlie approached. From the crowd, a voice called out:

'Somebody do something!'

But nobody did anything. Stanley was astonished to

see Abel stand up tall, and stick out his chin. He was even more amazed to see him raise two thin, pale hands, bunched into weedy little fists.

'Do your worst!' he snarled at Charlie.

'Alright!' said Charlie. He ducked down to gather up a handful of his dropped swag, and then rushed at Abel. The fainting lady fainted for real this time. Stanley instinctively grabbed a bun from a nearby waiter's tray and threw it at Charlie, to no effect.

Rasmussen shouted, 'Look – a lion!' but no one was fooled.

Stanley watched, in slow motion, what appeared to be Abel's inevitable end. But suddenly from the corner of his eye, he saw a blur. Something moved impossibly quickly, with a kind of whooshing sound, and then Charlie was fighting for his life. Somehow, between Charlie and Abel, had come Fassbinder, the jowly faced guest. He had no sword of his own, but he was jinking and swaying, avoiding Charlie's every attempt to hit him, and leading him away from Abel. He spun on a heel, and Charlie swung at him, but he was no longer there – he poked Charlie in the nose, and slipped away, while Charlie grew crosser and crosser. He swung more wildly, which only served to make Fassbinder's movements seem yet more graceful.

At one point the onlookers thought Charlie had made contact, a swift stab towards Fassbinder's right

eye, but no, Fassbinder was still moving fluidly. He was trying to wear Charlie down, and it was working. If Charlie tried to turn away, back towards the crowd or towards Abel, there was Fassbinder, standing on his foot. If Charlie attacked more forcefully, Fassbinder seemed to melt away almost to nothing, before coming back at Charlie with a wedgie or a tickle. Eventually it became like a dance, and the audience started treating it as an entertainment. The band even struck up, and the crowd began to clap along, which only made Charlie yet more cross. But eventually he slumped to the ground, and threw his remaining swag down in front of him. 'Here, take it!' he yelped. 'I don't want it any more. Just make him stop embarrassing me!'

The crowd yelped wildly, and a few burly crew members stood Charlie up. Fassbinder was gathered back into the throng, where Stanley heard him being suitably self-deprecating about his abilities. Behind them, Abel was apparently coming round from his concussion, to find himself he knew not where, being clapped on the back by revellers.

'Erm . . .?' he said, to no one. 'Did I say . . . do your worst?' and he sat down heavily on a chair.

'Will you take him to the Captain?' said Stanley, now standing by Charlie.

'No need,' said Rasmussen, pointing to the open doorway. There, accompanied by Clamdigger, who had run off to get him at the first sign of trouble, was the Captain. His greatcoat had been cleaned and pressed, his moustache was looking extra shiny, but he was still the same Captain, in his second-best hat. He took in the scene grimly, before his eyes rested in turn on Abel, Charlie, and then Mr Fassbinder.

'My apologies,' he rumbled, 'to the Gallooniers. I apologise for being absent once more in a crisis. To our guests, I apologise for this unseemly to-do. It is many years since crime was known aboard the Galloon.'

He approached the little group holding Charlie, and spoke quietly to his face.

'You will be provided with transport to leave. You will go home to your mother and make a new life for yourself. Be diligent and honest. Do good where you can. Stop making excuses. One day you may return and I will see about offering you a berth. Go.'

Some people in the crowd gasped, and some murmured disapprovingly, but Charlie himself just gulped quietly, and walked from the room, followed by Clamdigger. Stanley and Rasmussen looked at each other, and Rasmussen shrugged. Stanley saw Ms Huntley, who had been dancing away with the best of them, shed a single tear.

The Captain turned once more to the throng. 'We all owe thanks to Mr Fassbinder, and of course to our own Skyman Abel. Heroic efforts both.'

Stanley looked at the bewildered Skyman Abel, who seemed to grow in stature once again with this praise. He even stood up and bowed, though he quickly clutched his head and sat down again. Fassbinder waved a hand humbly, and sat down amongst his new admirers.

'Please!' called the Captain over the rising hubbub. 'Do not let this stop us enjoying the party. To the Count's birthday!'

'To the Count's birthday!' cried the crowd, many of whom had now found their glasses, snacks and dancing partners once again.

Stanley turned to Rasmussen, who was watching the Captain move through the crowd.

'So we weren't quick enough on this occasion, but it turned out alright in the end,' he said, draining a glass of juice he had just taken from a tray.

'Did it?' said Rasmussen. 'You know, I'm sure he got him in the eye. It went "clink". And how can he move like that? And what's that Skyman Abel's reading? Why did he say spy instead of thief? Lots of questions still to answer.'

'Clink?' said Stanley. Then: 'Perhaps he's a dancer. A note of some kind. His brain was mixed up,' to each of Rasmussen's questions in turn. He looked across the room to where Abel was now standing up, holding a piece of paper in each hand.

'Erm . . . Captain?' Abel was calling. 'You'd better see this. And you, Ms Huntley . . .'

'I'm so sorry, Jack, I've been a fool, I really have,' Charlie was saying, as he was being fastened into the boatswain's chair by Clamdigger.

'You have,' said Clamdigger seriously. 'But you have another chance. Use it.'

'I will. I will. He's a good man, that Captain.'

'He is that. Mind how you go, Charlie, and no more of this nonsense,' said Clamdigger, swaying Charlie out over the side of the Galloon before taking to the winch handle once more.

'That Fassbinder can move like no one else I've ever met. It didn't seem human. Do you know the scariest thing?' called Charlie, as he descended into the fog.

'No, what's that?'

'I thought I'd killed him. I could have sworn I stuck him in the eye!'

And with that, Charlie was gone.

GOODNIGHT!

A short while later, things were almost back in full swing. The Count was at the centre of a circle of well-wishers, and Stanley heard him saying he had never known such a happy birthday as this. The Bilgepump Orchestra was playing some slower, more soulful numbers, and the lighting had dimmed slightly – the party was entering its second phase, as night drew in over the mountains outside.

But Stanley and Rasmussen were not relaxing. After the drama of the foiled robbery, they had watched as the Captain and Ms Huntley had read the two notes, one from Cloudier and one from Fishbane. The Captain's face was hard to read at any time, but it was clear to Stanley that whatever was in the note had caused Ms Huntley some concern. She frowned and shot a glance at the Captain that could almost be called disapproving. Stanley guessed, correctly as it later turned out, that Cloudier had gone off on a mission of her own. The Captain and the Chief Navigator had had a whispered conflab as soon as they had read the note, and then Ms Huntley had hurried away, Stanley knew not where. From that moment, the ball had, to all appearances, gone on untroubled by events. But there was an undercurrent of unease, and Stanley and Rasmussen made it their business to find out what was going on. Stanley continued to dance, and also to help people to snacks and drinks, and he found that this was a great way to eavesdrop and gauge the mood of the room.

'Tiny pie, sir? Volly-vont, madam?' he said to a table full of mixed ball guests, who were busy chatting away.

'I simply haven't seen him since before we left Eisberg,' the Count was saying slightly blurrily.

'He'll come home when he's hungry,' brayed a toothy man in a flappy hat.

'He's a valet, man, not a lapdog!'

'Yes – not nearly so loyal!' replied flappy hat, and Stanley was pleased to see the Count turn his back on this unpleasant man and engage his neighbour. Stanley moved on.

'Kweesh?' he said to a group standing by the dance floor.

'He moved like no one I've ever seen,' a lady in a long black dress was saying. 'Almost inhuman!'

She was shushed by her friends as Fassbinder walked past, so Stanley assumed he was the cause of her amazement. Someone took a piece of quiche from Stanley, then he popped the tray down on a table, and hurried over to where Rasmussen was pouring fizzy water for a table of parlour maids.

'Mr Pill the valet's still missing, and Fassbinder's the talk of the town . . .' he reported.

'Shh!' said Rasmussen. She was clearly listening to the parlour maids' chatter.

'My Bert's cousin Fred lives onboard the Galloon,' one was saying with a kind of urgent glee. 'And he says that the anchormen have been called away – which must mean we're going to be on the move!'

'On the move?' said another. 'But the party's still going on! We can't . . .'

'We can,' interrupted Rasmussen, 'if the Captain wants to.'

She turned to Stanley and continued.

'I think he planned to wait until tomorrow to head off, but something in those letters persuaded him to move more quickly. No one here will even notice unless they go outside, and no doubt we can be back here in time for everyone to be on their way soon enough,' she said, moving round the table filling glasses.

'So I recommend that we keep our ears to the ground, our noses to the grindstone, our eyes peeled, and our mouths shut,' said Stanley. 'Adventure will make itself known soon enough no doubt.'

'What are we looking out for?' said Rasmussen absently.

'Well, I don't think that Charlie stealing things was what Abel was talking about – he must have read something in those notes about a spy onboard. So we should look out for anything untoward, I suppose.'

'Like one of the more mysterious ball guests looking shiftily around the room as he edges towards the door, then slipping quietly out, as if he doesn't want to be noticed?' said Rasmussen.

'Yes, that kind of thing,' agreed Stanley. 'If that happened, we'd be duty bound to follow him, whatever the risks, on a knife-edge journey into the unknown with the future of the very Galloon itself at stake,' said Stanley thoughtfully.

'Yes, I agree,' said Rasmussen, sipping a cup of tea she had somehow managed to conjure up. 'And hopefully, once that's done, we'll be free to keep an eye out for this adventure we've been waiting for.'

'Hear hear,' said Stanley, but Rasmussen's attention was already elsewhere.

'Look over there,' she said.

Stanley turned and watched, as Mr Fassbinder, who was standing by himself, apparently admiring a pot plant, began to shift edgily towards the main doors of the ballroom. He looked around the room as he did so, but didn't notice Stanley and Rasmussen. He opened the door a crack with his fingertips, and then stood quietly in front of it for a couple of moments, as if he just happened to prefer standing by doors. Then he swung it open enough for his lithe frame to fit through, and was gone in a blink.

'Corks,' said Stanley.

'That's what we've been looking for,' said Rasmussen. 'What reason could he have for going out that way?'

'He could be . . .' began Stanley, ever literal.

'Shush, please!' said Rasmussen. 'He could have many reasons, legitimate or otherwise. Let's follow him on a knife-edge journey into the unknown to find out.'

'With the very future of the Galloon at stake?' said Stanley excitedly.

'Well, I don't know yet, do I?' Rasmussen smiled. 'But there's only one way to find out.'

And she slurped her teacup empty, plonked it on the table and stood up.

'To the kitchens!' she said.

'Oh,' said Stanley. 'That's not what I expected . . .' But he followed her anyway.

Cloudier was cold. Not tingly fingers and steamy breath cold, but blue lips and stabbing-pains-in-the-joints cold. Breathing was a chore, and her eyes streamed, with the tears freezing on her cheeks almost immediately. She had actually dropped quite a long way since leaving the Galloon, following valleys and passes rather than trying to float over the Eisberg Mountains as the Galloon itself could do, but the cold was still much worse than she could ever have imagined. It was only the occasional blast from the burner that gave her any warmth at all, but that couldn't be used too much, as it would send her floating higher, into even colder air.

She had blankets, and gloves, and a flask of tea that Clamdigger had made for her, but she was beginning to feel foolish for setting out on her own, Captain's orders or no. She hoped that someone had paid attention to her message, but even if they had she knew they'd be unlikely to follow until morning. So she pulled the blankets closer round her shoulders, and peered again over the edge of the basket, into the gloaming.

Flying her little balloon out over the sea in the dead of night, heading for an island range of fiery volcanoes where the Captain's sworn enemy could be waiting.

She didn't mind – she'd have jumped out of the balloon here and now if it would save the Galloon – but she did wish she'd brought a friend along for company. Someone to share the experience with. Cloudier was aware that an adventure undertaken alone wasn't a proper adventure until you were back home, repeating it to a circle of friends round a cosy fire. If she did get back, of course . . .

She shook off these dark thoughts, while also logging them for future poetic reference. She resolved to keep a journal of her adventures, so that if she never saw Clamdi— anyone again, there was still a chance that her exploits would be known.

With this in mind, she held her trusty pen up to the burner. The ink was frozen, and it was a delicate matter to unfreeze it, and her fingers, enough to do some writing, without sending the balloon too high up into the air. She was very proud of the little craft so far, but she was aware that conditions were calm and there could be sterner tests head. Once the pen had warmed a little, she shook it by her ear and heard the ink sploshing about. This done, she balanced her trusty notebook on the edge of the Galloon, and with the controlling ropes of the balloon in one hand, she managed to flip it open, manoeuvre the pen into a comfortable position and write.

Dear Diary,

she wrote, and then felt self-conscious. She scribbled it out and began again.

It's cold. I am high up. I could really use a fry-up . . .

No, stick to prose.

I am alone, but then are we not all alone? I am up in the air, but then, who is not up in the air, in some way? I fly into the unknown, but then who does not . . .

No. She was annoying herself already. Try not to try so hard . . .

Cloudier's log, two hours out from GG. The dusk is beautiful – snow falling in fat white flakes, fog still close, an eerie calm. But very aware of the importance of my journey. If I can find the Sumbaroon, and follow it, or get a message back to the Captain, then his quest to reclaim his lost love and save the precious Galloon may be in its final stages. If I fail, then Zebediah's deceit will be complete, and the Galloon will once again be in peril. The balloon responds well. I cannot see much, but the ground is in sight, and the fog seems to be lifting.

Cloudier stopped for a moment, to shake her stiff hand, and then continued.

I think I can just make out the line of the sea ahead, beyond the foothills. From there it shouldn't be too far to the Chimney Isles. I'll arrive in the early hours. I will keep this journal up as long as the cold allows.

Cloudier thought she heard a sound on the wind – the scree-kakkk-kakkk-kakkk noise of a Seagle. But it was distant, and lost in the fog.

I feel as if Fishbane, or one of his people, is

following me. This is reassuring, as long as he doesn't poo all over this journal and render it useless. But then again, perhaps it's just the mountain winds.

She heard the noise again, however this time it sounded like it could have been a wolf howling in the distant forests. She steeled herself and carried on writing.

It's nice to finally have some time on my own, without any grown-ups interfering and sticking their silly noses in everywhere. To be in charge of my destiny, just me and the open skies. To be mistress of my own universe, with no one telling me what I can and can't do . . .

She re-read this, and then thought of her mother reading it, and being upset. She drew a thick line through it all and wrote:

If I can't be honest with a diary, what's the point?

She swallowed and carried on.

I wish my mum was here.

101

And she looked up at the darkening horizon, where the foothills gave way to the waves.

Rasmussen had, within moments of leaving the ball-room, ceased to look like a little puffball princess, and become her usual, slightly grubby self. Her dress was intact but somehow deflated, and all extraneous ribbons, bows, rosettes, ringlets and jewellery had been jettisoned. Stanley felt much more comfortable, as she strode along beside him, occasionally hiding behind a pillar for no more reason than because it felt like the kind of thing you should do when following someone.

Fassbinder was turning out to be a challenge to follow and impossible to second-guess. Stanley and Rasmussen had rushed through the little kitchen near the ballroom, where much of the prep for the party was happening, and had hopped into a dumb waiter, which took them up one deck. Then they had crept along the corridor that ran over the ballroom, hoping to catch Fassbinder coming up the stairs at the far end, on his way to the main deck.

They couldn't think exactly what it was he would be up to, but it seemed likely that, as he didn't know his way around the Galloon, that would be his starting point. But of course he hadn't been there, and they had crept around stealthily but pointlessly for a good few minutes, whistling like owls and signalling to each other, before realising he was nowhere to be seen. They had panicked a little, and thought about giving it all up, before Stanley caught a glimpse of him rushing down a staircase that only really led to a broom cupboard. They had realised that, of course, Fassbinder might be a master spy, but he had no idea where he was going, so they hit upon another tactic. Grabbing a cape and hat from the cloakroom nearby, they had waited at the top of the spiral staircase, knowing Fassbinder had to emerge soon, unless his secret mission was to tidy the broom cupboard, in which case good luck to him.

Before too long, Fassbinder had of course climbed the stairs, silently and seemingly with no embarrassment. He had found, at the top of the stairs, a moustachioed gent in a cape and hat, and so he had asked the way to the Captain's cabin. The gent (who was of course Rasmussen with her ponytail stretched under her nose, standing on Stanley's shoulders) had thought for a moment before giving him detailed directions in the silliest accent Stanley had ever heard. The gent had then seemingly giggled a little around the midriff, before recovering his composure as Fassbinder moved on.

And so now, they were following Fassbinder through the familiar corridors of the Galloon, and were able to keep a reasonable distance because they already had a good idea of where he was going.

'Why do you think he wants to go the Captain's

cabin?' whispered Stanley, from beneath the large pile of clothes they had borrowed from the cloakroom, in case of the need for more disguises.

'I'm not sure,' said Rasmussen, struggling to control the pile of dresses and wigs in her arms.

'Perhaps he wants to talk to the Captain?' mused Stanley.

'The Captain was at the dance, he could have talked to him at any point. There's something much more untoward going on.'

They hurried on in silence for a while, stopping to peer round corners, and leaving just enough of a distance between Fassbinder and themselves so as not to make him suspicious. He disappeared down a hatchway, which Stanley knew led to the corridor where the Captain's cabin was situated.

'Come,' said Rasmussen, who knew the ins and outs of the Galloon even better than Stanley, having lived aboard it all her life.

She turned to the left and began to feel around the edges of what seemed to Stanley to be a perfectly ordinary plank, part of the wall panelling that ran along the inside of most of the below-deck spaces on the Galloon.

It turned out it was a perfectly ordinary plank, so Stanley watched patiently as Rasmussen tried another, then another, and finally a third.

'Maybe . . .' he said, but she interrupted immediately.

'Watch and learn, Mr Furry!' she said pompously, as the third plank proved to be loose. She pulled it out with a 'squeak', and thrust her head into the gap created. Then she squeezed her shoulders in, and the rest of her. Stanley watched as she climbed down the gap between the panelling and the walls proper.

'Used to be some piping or something in here, but now it's a handy shortcut. Follow me!' she said, lowering herself further into the hole, and dragging the ragged selection of dressing-up clothes with her.

Stanley followed, and was surprised to see that, through this hidden gap, they had access to the floor below. He waited for Rasmussen to get through and began to push his own pile of clothes into the hole. He heard them drop to the ground below. Then he squeezed through, and hung by his fingers before dropping himself. Looking about, he realised that they were in the corridor near the Captain's cabin, and had got there a good deal quicker than Fassbinder.

'Put these on!' said Rasmussen. 'He's coming!'

Unthinkingly, Stanley threw himself into all the clothes Rasmussen handed him. It was only afterwards that he realised he was wearing an apron dress with a number of pinafores and underskirts, a little lace bonnet, and a handbag.

'I look like a milkmaid!' he complained to Rasmussen, but she was nowhere to be seen. In her place was an upstanding young guardsman, clean faced but stern, with a smartly pressed uniform and a steely gaze.

'Rasmussen?' he said, looking around in bewilderment.

'It's me, you turnip!' said the guardsman. 'It's a disguise. Ten per cent costume, ten per cent luck, and ninety per cent belief. If you believe it, he'll believe it!'

'But that makes more than a hundred per cent,' complained Stanley, still in awe. Now he looked, of course it was obvious that Rasmussen was standing before him, dressed in a long grey coat and a tall shako hat, standing on top, rather than in, a pair of black boots. She lifted up a foot, and showed him that each boot was stuffed with spare clothing.

'A hundred per cent isn't enough!' hissed Rasmussen as footsteps approached along the corridor. 'You have to have more than that to make it work.'

'But you can't have more . . .' replied Stanley, however his sentence was cut short by Fassbinder, who rounded the corner and stopped dead. He seemed, for the first time, to be surprised.

'Ah! Young man, madam, good day . . .' he said, filling time.

For the first time Stanley wondered why he couldn't have been the soldier, and let Rasmussen be the milkmaid. But it was too late now. Rasmussen was staring blankly at the opposite wall, in true soldierly style, so Stanley piped up.

'Lor, fie I say, as I was a-walking one morning in Maytime . . .' he said inexplicably.

The soldier gave him a look.

'Quite,' said Fassbinder. 'I wonder if either of you could tell me which is the Captain's cabin. He's a good friend of mine and I wanted a quick word . . .'

'CAPTAIN'S IN THE BALLROOOOOOM, *SAH!*' screamed Rasmussen, at the very top of her surprisingly loud voice.

'Aha!' said Fassbinder, stepping back a little. 'Then perhaps I could just slip in and leave a note on his desk?'

'Deary my oh lordy, fol-de-rol diddle and bless my soul!' said Stanley, whose only experience of milkmaids came from folk songs.

'It's this door, is it?' said Fassbinder, his tone just beginning to betray impatience.

'CAPTAIN'S PUH-RIVATE CABIN IS THIS DOOR WHAT I AM A-STANDING BY OF, SIR YES SIR, *SAH!*' bawled Rasmussen, clearly enjoying herself immensely.

'So if I can just . . .' said Fassbinder, stepping round Rasmussen, who of course couldn't move easily owing to standing on piles of clothing stuffed into boots many sizes too big for her.

'I'm not sure we can—' said Stanley, before remembering himself. 'Oh, my handsome soldier, my dainty duck, my dear-o. Are we sure we should be . . .?'

But before he could finish the thought, and to his dismay, Fassbinder was stepping past Rasmussen, and into the Captain's cabin, his private study, which was, for some reason, unlocked.

Once in, he leaned out of the door, and spoke to Rasmussen the soldier.

'Let me know if anyone's coming, won't you, old boy? I'd hate to . . . spoil the surprise.'

'RIGHT YOU ARE, SAH! YOU'LL FIND ME THE VERY SOUL OF DISCRETIOOOOOOOOOOOOO-OOON . . . *SAH!*' screamed Rasmussen, saluting, winking, nodding her head and, somehow, clicking her heels all at once.

This was too much for her disguise, which fell apart around her, but no matter, as Fassbinder was now inside the Captain's cabin, with the door firmly shut. They even heard him bolt the door from the inside.

'Now what do we do!?' whispered Stanley urgently. 'Why did you let him go in?'

'BECAUSE . . . I mean because . . .' began Rasmussen, moderating her voice as she remembered where she was. 'Because, if we don't let him in, he may turn nasty, and he'll just try and come back later. But if we let him in, we can retire to our trusty hidey-hole in the ceiling above the Captain's study, and see exactly what he's up to.'

As she said this, she began to climb the walls of the corridor. By bracing her back against one wall, and her legs against the other, she edged her way up to a beam above Stanley's head. Once it was in reach, she grabbed it, and used it to clamber into a tiny space, only a few inches high, between the top of the door and the beam. Stanley knew of this hidey-hole, as they had used it before, so it was the work of a moment to clamber up and join her in the musty little space.

Rasmussen pulled aside a small piece of wood that covered a gap in the floor of the tight space, and then Stanley was looking down on Fassbinder, standing in the middle of the Captain's snug study. He stood for a few seconds, just looking around, without moving. Stanley did too, but from where he was squatting, he could only see all the room's normal bric-a-brac. A green-leather-topped desk, brass firedogs, a washstand and basin, a few seats and a hat stand. A suit of armour in one corner, two small pot plants, and a mantelpiece on which Stanley knew the Captain kept a portrait of Isabella, his life's true love and the focus of his quest.

As they watched, cramming their faces together to look through the hole, Stanley and Rasmussen couldn't help but feel that something had changed in Fassbinder's demeanour. He moved in a slightly clunkier manner as

110

he began to move around the room, and all pretence at grace was gone now he wasn't on show any more. To their dismay, he swiped a hand across the Captain's desk, knocking inkstand, lamp and clock to the floor. He wrenched open a desk drawer, before turning it over so that all the contents fell on the floor. He stood for a second looking at the debris, then opened another drawer, scanned the upturned contents, and carried on with a third. Whatever he was looking for didn't seem to be in there, so he continued to the other side of the desk, and began to turn those drawers over as well.

In their cubbyhole, Stanley and Rasmussen looked at each other in shock – this was more serious than they had thought.

'We shouldn't be watching this,' whispered Stanley. 'We should stop him!'

'Yes,' said Rasmussen. 'But you saw him in the ballroom – he's too fast and skilful for us tackle him head on. We must think of another plan.'

They put their heads to the hole again while they thought. Stanley watched as Fassbinder took a piece of paper from his pocket, and held it up to the light from the small fire, which was still burning in the grate. Stanley squinted and, next to him, he heard Rasmussen say, 'What is that?'

What was on the paper was a picture – something the shape of a half-moon, and the size of a side plate.

111

Drawn in charcoal, in a style that could be described as 'scruffy'. But then Stanley slapped himself on the forehead, carefully avoiding his blunt little horn, which was quite capable of giving him a bruise. He turned to Rasmussen, and made the sign in their secret sign language for 'lost love token'.

'Lost love token!' said Rasmussen aloud.

'Yes!' signed Stanley.

'Pardon?' signed Rasmussen.

'Yes!' signed Stanley, more clearly.

'Pardon?' signed Rasmussen.

'Yes!' Stanley signed again. 'Lost love token.'

'I get the "lost love token" bit, but what was the other thing you were saying?' whispered Rasmussen.

'It was just "yes"!' said Stanley.

'No, this is "yes",' said Rasmussen impatiently.

'No, that's "Zombie Pirate King",' said Stanley. '*This* is "yes".'

'Oh. I thought *that* was "excuse me please, which way to the post office?",' said Rasmussen.

'Well, it's not,' said Stanley. 'Please can we concentrate – look!'

They looked back down the hole, and Stanley saw to his dismay that Fassbinder was now walking – lurching almost, for some reason – towards the mantelpiece. He still had the piece of paper in his hand, and it was clear now that this was a rubbing, a direct copy, of Isabella's half of the love token the Captain had once given her. Fassbinder was looking for the Captain's half!

'He dropped it down a chimney,' said Stanley. 'I mean a volcano! In the Chimney Islands!'

'Ssshhh!' said Rasmussen.

Fassbinder looked up, almost as if he had heard something. Stanley's heart was in his mouth, as the man below them cocked an ear, but then he went back to walking towards the mantelpiece.

'What's he doing?' said Rasmussen, who couldn't quite see through the hole as well as Stanley.

'He's picking up the portrait of the Captain's bride!' said Stanley, in awe.

Rasmussen gasped, and tried to stand, before remembering where they were and lying down again.

'We have to stop him! Let's go in there!' she said.

'Yes!' said Stanley. 'We'll go in and . . . and . . .'

At a loss, he put his eye to the hole again.

'What's happening?' said Rasmussen by his ear.

'He's got Isabella in his hand. He's turning the picture over, looking for something on the back. He's . . . he's *breaking it*! He's taking the back off! He's smashed the glass and the frame onto the floor! He's found . . . a piece of paper! He's opening it up. It's a map! Hidden in the back of the frame! It says . . . It says . . .'

'What does it say? What does it say?' shouted Rasmussen, all pretence at quietness gone.

113

'It says "The Kraken's Lair!" next to a picture of a big volcano amongst lots of islands. I think that's it; I think that's where the love token is!'

'What love token?' yelped Rasmussen, who hated not being in the know.

'The one the Captain split in half and gave one bit of to Isabella as a token of undying love but then dropped down a volcano by accident.'

'Tsk. Boys.' Rasmussen rolled her eyes. Stanley ignored her.

'And now he's . . . he's taking his eye out!'

There was a moment of silence.

'He's what now?' said Rasmussen calmly.

'He's taken it right out and he's pointing it at the map!' Stanley heard a click and saw a brief flash of light as he said this. 'It's not an eye, it's some sort of device like a little camera or something.'

Down in the room, a puff of smoke and a flash had emitted from Fassbinder's disconnected eye, and he held it in his hand for a moment before putting it back in place. This meant he had a momentary blind spot on his left side, so he didn't see what Stanley saw, which was that the suit of armour in the corner of the room had begun to move. At first just one glove, as if to shield the eyes from the flash of light, but then, as Fassbinder went to throw the little canvas portrait of Isabella Croucher into the fire, the whole suit moved

114

more quickly than would have seemed possible a moment before.

The great metal thing appeared to bend at the knees, and Stanley heard a guttural roar, amplified and distorted by the metal, as the suit leapt forward and over the desk towards Fassbinder. He noticed a second too late, and despite his cat-like reflexes, the suit of armour got to him before he could move out of the way.

Stanley was now too gobsmacked to give a running commentary, and Rasmussen had her eye back at the spy hole. Together they gawped as the suit of armour thrust a fist into the fire and caught the little portrait just as it landed on the hot coals. Another roar came from the visor, and Stanley was yet more amazed to see the other glove go to the suit's visor, and raise it with a clang. For inside the suit of armour was the Captain! His face was twisted with anger and pain, but he had saved the portrait from the flames. He stood up quickly, and wrenched the scorched glove from his hand.

Fassbinder seemed to be frozen to the spot – but only for a second. Tucking the map into a pocket, he ran for the door. The Captain lunged for him, but he was already away, so it was all the Captain could do to fling the metal gauntlet in his direction.

'Zebediah is behind this!' he roared, and began to

heave and tug at the suit of armour, trying to get out of it so he could give proper chase to the spy.

Behind Stanley, Rasmussen peeped over the edge of the little cubbyhole, and Stanley heard her say, 'He's heading for the main deck!' Then she began to clamber down. Stanley followed her, swinging down from the beam just as the Captain noticed Rasmussen entering his office.

'What the . . .?' he shouted, then, more quietly. 'Are you hurt, girl?'

'No, sir,' said Rasmussen. 'He's heading for the deck.'

'Help me with me boots, damn them. Stanley! You too. By gad, you two have your fingers in every pie.'

'He's got . . .'

'I know, lad! He belongs to my brother, curse his liver and lights! I'm making chase. Warn the others!'

'Can't we use the speaking tubes, sir?' said Stanley, as they left the office, the suit of armour now lying on the floor by the fire.

'Only from the quarterdeck, Stanley. No tannoy down here, though perhaps there should be. But if I can't beat an interloper in a race against time onboard me own ship, I don't deserve to. You coming?'

Stanley observed, as he had been lucky enough to observe in the past, that the Captain's face seemed to come alive at times like this – his eyes twinkled, his laughter lines crinkled, and he seemed to be truly himself, despite the grim set to his face. He also, Stanley knew from experience, showed a healthy disregard for the usual rules of responsible adult behaviour. He had been happy in the past for Stanley to risk his life in the name of adventure, and he seemed to be happy to do so again as he swept away, down the corridor that led back towards the deck.

'Yup!' shouted Rasmussen, sweeping after him, though unable to produce quite the same effect, as she was a young girl in a ripped pink ball gown, rather than a huge and imposing man in a greatcoat and a tricorn hat. Stanley stopped for a moment to marvel at the fact that the Captain had had these things with him even when hiding inside a suit of armour, before running after them. He was just in time to see them disappearing round a corner, and to hear the Captain shouting, 'For the Galloon!' and Rasmussen replying with the traditional, 'And for the Captain!' He put on a burst of speed, and found them standing in a corridor, with the Captain kicking at the skirting board.

'Did we lose him?' he asked breathlessly.

'Not likely!' said the Captain, and began to heave and wrench at a wall panel.

'Are any of these walls real?' said Rasmussen, impressed.

'Of course!' said the Captain. 'About half, I'd say. Follow me!'

And he disappeared up the spiral staircase that had been revealed behind the false panel. Stanley was surprised to see that it was made of stone.

'Took it from a castle I was laying siege to,' called the Captain, as if reading his mind. 'Thought I might as well make use of it. Leads straight up to the deck now.'

And with a hearty laugh that made Stanley's heart glad, he rushed on up the stairs, after the mysterious interloper.

A following wind has helped my progress, while blowing the flesh from my bones, it seems. I am cold down to my very soul, and only Clamdigger's flask is keeping me from freezing up like a block of ice, I'm sure. The fog has blown off now, as I approach the sea. The tang of salt is in the air. And something else – sulphur? Usually I would attribute this to Fishbane and his pongy poos, but he is nowhere around. Perhaps it is a sign that I will soon be over the Chimney Isles.

And then what?

I will find the token, of course. A small thing I have never seen, lost in a landscape of fire-belching volcanoes, while piloting a hot air balloon, in sub-zero temperatures, over an unknown sea.

Cloudier suddenly felt very small and young. She peeped over the edge of the balloon, at the line of the islands, now visible as a grey shadow on the horizon. She saw that at that very moment she was passing over the coastline, from the mountainous wilds of the Countship of Eisberg, to the Great Northern Ocean. She was past the point of no return. She couldn't land, and the wind would not let her turn back.

Squinting at the sea, she was surprised to see that the ice was not solid – currents must have kept it moving, for it was a heaving mixture of ice and slush, whipped up in parts to a froth by the fast winds. Ice floes, varying in size from dining table to football pitch, were dotted around. The occasional berg – mountains of ice that she knew would shine blue in the sun, but which now looked like forbidding shadows – floated by below.

She passed a few moments by picking out bergs that looked familiar. There was one that had a look of Mr Wouldbegood about it. Another looked a little like Claude, his great wings outstretched. And that one there, a long, low shape, quite unlike the others, could almost be . . . well, it looked like it even had a small human shape on its back . . . and a periscope . . . it really did look uncannily like . . .

The Grand Sumbaroon of Zebediah Anstruther!

Cloudier goggled. She squinted. She looked at it askance.

There could be no doubt. Now her eyes were becoming accustomed to the distance and the darkness, there could be no doubt whatsoever. There, moored to the only rock that broke the surface, half submerged in the slushy sea, was the dread conveyance of the Captain's no-good brother. A kind of lumpy sausage of rivets and metal panels, it had none of the grace of the Galloon, and was a fraction of the size, but nevertheless it was a fearsome machine, and nobody knew exactly what it was capable of.

Cloudier watched as a tiny figure, risking its life in these conditions, clambered about on the top of the Sumbaroon, apparently erecting some kind of flagpole or mast. Cloudier understood this was important – she had to let the Captain know of this development, and luckily she had a way of doing so. With unwilling fingers, she fumbled about under the little table in her balloon, and pulled out one of the message-shaped capsules she had used so often before. But this one was slightly different. Clamdigger had been fiddling with it, and instead of a clip to attach the capsule to a rope, there was a small pair of wings, made of thin canvas stretched over a wire frame. Struggling to even hold the pen now, Cloudier managed to scratch out a desperate message on a page of her journal.

The Sumbaroon is here. I am watching and will follow. Three hours west, in a bay of ice, by a rock that looks like Abel's hat. Come if you can.
C
P.S. Tell Mum I've still got my gloves on.

She managed to scrumple the note up, and stuff it into the capsule. The key for the clockwork mechanism had iced up, but by breathing on it she managed to free it enough to wind it. She counted ten turns – a wild guess, but the best she could do. Holding the wings still, she held the capsule up into the wind, and then she let go. The wing beats were surprisingly strong, and with only a little trouble, the thing began making headway, back the way they had come, like a crazed butterfly on migration.

Clamdigger had assured her that it would fly straight and true, and as far as she could work out she had travelled more or less due west from the Galloon. But it seemed like a hopeless shot in the dark to think that it would find its way home. In desperation, she managed to scribble out a copy of the note, stuff it into another capsule, the only other one modified in this way, and then she released that one too.

Her fingers aching with the effort, and every sensible part of her brain screaming at her to lie down in the bottom of the basket with a blanket over her head, she nevertheless managed to force herself to face front again. She began to seek out a safe place to moor the balloon – she couldn't risk being blown straight past, and losing sight of it forever. She let warm air out of the top of it, making it drop towards the ocean, and then gave it a burst of the burner, just in case she had let out too much.

She felt fairly assured that the Sumbaroon would not have seen her, dark against the night sky and unlooked for, but she knew that she had to be very careful indeed. So she piloted the balloon towards one of the larger ice floes, that would allow her to see about half of the Sumbaroon sticking out from behind the distinctive Abel-hat rock, without itself being visible to the Sumbaroon's periscope. That way she would know if it moved off, and be able to take off again, without risking her own safety too much.

She chuckled wryly to herself as she realised that 'not risking her own safety too much' meant, in this context, landing a hot air balloon on an ice floe within sight of a mortal enemy. She had been flying quite low over the ocean, and so it was only a matter of a few moments before the little balloon crunched down onto the ice, rocking dangerously as it did so.

Cloudier heaved the small iron anchor overboard, and was satisfied to see that it stuck fast in the ice without going through. She had to stay alert – keeping just enough hot air in the balloon to stop it deflating and flopping down onto the ice, from where it would be difficult to refill, but not so much that she actually took off or put any strain on the anchor.

With this delicate balancing act underway, she squinted through the gloom, to where the Sumbaroon's nose was just visible poking out from behind Abel's Hat Rock, as she had decided to name it. The periscope was indeed out of sight behind the rock, but to her dismay the man who she had seen climbing about on top of the vessel was now directly in her line of vision, and so she in his. He seemed preoccupied, however.

His bulbous shape, no doubt wrapped in furs and cloaks against the battering winds, appeared to be wrestling with a contraption of some kind. Was he setting up a flagpole? A windsock? Some long thin article, constantly caught by the wind and almost whipped from his hands, was causing him trouble as he tried to manhandle it into an unseen post hole on the deck. Cloudier wished she'd brought her binoculars. Was it an aerial? A mast of some kind? Impossible to know. All she could do was watch, and stay alert, and hope that at least one of her messages made it to the Captain in time . . .

The Captain, Stanley and Rasmussen had burst out onto the deck, to find the night had drawn in, and every square inch of sky visible beyond and around the great sails and balloons was filled with stars. The winds appeared to have seen the fog off completely, and Stanley saw that the Galloon was indeed underway, no longer moored up to Castle Eisberg.

'I had them weigh anchor!' yelled the Captain over his shoulder, as he ran along the deck with great strides that Stanley and Rasmussen couldn't hope to match. 'I may not exactly have permission to search, but now I have the Count on my side, I feel our time is best used in making for the Chimney Isles. With this wind, we'll be over the coast in no time. And then we make for the Kraken's Lair!'

As he said this, he was loping along the deck, occasionally leaping a kennel or dodging round a rainwater barrel. Stanley and Rasmussen were beginning to fall behind, but they knew there was no way the Captain could slow down. Ahead of them, running just as quickly, and with his now customary litheness, Fassbinder was keeping his distance.

Many of the ball-goers had come out on deck to see the stars, and to marvel at the Galloon's stately progress, only to find themselves goggling as the chase unfolded. Gallooniers amongst them, and a few game guests, made attempts to stop Fassbinder in his tracks, but he was so well practised that even the famed skill and speed of the crew was not enough.

They watched as he leapt clean over Snivens, a man who was himself no mean opponent. Fassbinder then jinked round a huge crewman called Brassic, and leapt from a storage trunk over the head of a bewildered earl. Ahead of him, more and more people were emerging from the main hatch, and becoming aware of the furore. Stanley and Rasmussen, realising that this was the Captain's chase now, began to fall back, until a rattling and howling behind them caused them to turn round. Just as they did so, Clamdigger's dog cart, with four slobbering hounds out front, shot past them, and clattered to a halt.

'Onboard!' cried the cabin boy. 'He may need our help!'

Stanley and Rasmussen looked at each other, and Rasmussen actually clapped her hands with glee, as they clambered on. Immediately, Clamdigger shouted, 'On, boys!' The big grey dogs, straining at their harnesses, leapt away. Now they were outpacing everybody, and gaining on the Captain. Stanley saw him duck below a low hanging rope, and leap a hatchway, without breaking stride. Clamdigger swung the dog cart out wide to avoid these obstacles, and they were thundering along by the taffrail, with lords and ladies, maids and crewmembers scattering out of their way.

Fassbinder, perhaps because of his lack of familiarity with the Galloon, was falling back as the chase continued towards where the mainmast rose from the deck, twelve sturdy trunks lashed together in a bundle. He seemed to be looking for higher ground – he clambered up onto a pile of hammocks and rope that was neatly stashed amidships, and began reaching for the rigging overhead – but this gave the Captain precious moments to catch up.

As the interloper tried to swing himself up into the web of ropes and nets that attached the galloon to its gigantic bundle of balloons and sails, the Captain was almost on him, and Clamdigger's cart was coming up on the outside. With a triumphant roar, the Captain leapt in the air and grabbed a rope, hanging like a vine in the jungle. His impetus swung him forward, and he managed to scramble up a rope ladder quicker than seemed possible. Stanley couldn't help but shout out as the Captain, with a grace that belied his bulk, managed to get himself *above* Fassbinder. The spy seemed shocked to see the Captain rise above him like a tide, before they tumbled together to the deck.

'He's got him!' called Clamdigger, bringing the dog cart to a halt in a wide arc nearby. He leapt from the vehicle onto the deck, and Rasmussen and Stanley followed.

The Captain and Fassbinder were locked in a frantic tussle on the ground, and the mysterious stranger's athletic abilities were of little use to him now. The Captain wasn't some petty thief, trying to make a fast exit. He was the Captain, and he was fighting for his life, and for his lost love. There was nothing fancy about his style – he just held on.

Fassbinder tried to twist away, step aside, jink, swerve, flip and dazzle, but with the Captain's great hands clasped around each arm, there was simply nowhere to go. Stanley, Rasmussen and Clamdigger slowed down, aware that there was no help they could give at this point. Like all the other Gallooniers and guests gathering around the grappling pair, they could only stand and gape in awe. Something was happening to Fassbinder – his movements were becoming faster, jerkier, more unsettling to watch. Stanley was astonished to see smoke begin to emerge from his head, as he tried to shake, squirm or wrench himself free. The Captain himself had a look of horrified determination on his face. Stanley knew that merely catching fire would not be enough to save Fassbinder from his vice-like grip.

A noise began to emerge from Fassbinder, which Stanley at first thought was a scream. But no, as he listened it turned into a high-pitched buzzing, an angry mosquito of a sound. Stanley looked around for a moment, in fear of BeheMoths, but the noise was definitely coming from Fassbinder. He was now moving in an entirely mechanical fashion, his head oscillating like the bell on an alarm clock, his legs kicking like a mechanical donkey.

'Blimey,' said Rasmussen. 'He's been clockwork all along.'

'Eh?' said Stanley, before realisation dawned. While perhaps not clockwork as such, it was clear that Fassbinder was indeed an automaton of some sort. The Captain was now standing, holding the malfunctioning Fassbinder at arm's length, albeit no less securely. His ears now aflame, his head spinning like a top, and his feet poking out on springs, Fassbinder appeared to be no longer a threat. But he had one last trick up his sleeve. As his hair fell out in clumps, the false head fizzed loudly, and its layers of make-up and disguise began to peel off. First, the kindly laughter lines and jowls began to melt away, revealing a younger, smoother face beneath.

'Pill!' yelled the Count of Eisberg from the crowd. 'It was Pill, my bally valet all this time!'

But then the layers continued to melt, and another onlooker seemed to recognise the next identity to be revealed.

'Brandon, my chauffeur! I knew there was something strange about him,' called a man in a wide-brimmed hat. 'But to be fair, not quite this strange . . .'

The layers carried on disappearing, and now others seemed to recognise various unveiled identities of the mechanical man.

'Reginald! That's my first husband!' cried a tall lady with a lorgnette and no chin to speak of. 'I had no idea he was an . . . actually, I'm not surprised he was an automaton. Makes perfect sense. As you were.'

Then it was all over, as the head, now down to its bare structure of metal, popped off the artificial neck like a grasshopper. It flew up in the air, still spinning, and Stanley watched as the eye-camera which he had seen through the spy hole in the Captain's cabin flew out of its socket. As the head itself fell smoking to the floor, the eye-spy seemed to hover for a moment, getting its bearings, before a small aerial extended from it, with a flashing red light on the end. It just had time to emit a series of loud beeps, some sort of code possibly, before it too fell lifelessly to the deck, where it was gobbled up by one of Clamdigger's dogs.

'Good lord,' said the Sultana of Magrabor, breaking the spell somewhat.

'Stone the crows,' said an old retainer emphatically.

'Well, quite,' said the Captain, before collapsing,

exhausted, to the deck, his map of the Chimney Isles and the portrait of his lost love stuffed safely in his pocket.

GOODNIGHT!

A few minutes later, it seemed to Stanley that the Grand Winter Ball had simply decamped onto the deck of the Galloon, as festivities carried on regardless of the bitter cold, the Captain's indisposition, or the revelations of a robot spy so recently in their midst. The Captain himself had been firmly seated in a chair by the Countess of Hammerstein, with orders not to move until he had drained the cup of hot broth she had pressed into his hand. Extra torches and braziers had been lit around the deck, and blankets distributed, and now even the Bilgepump Orchestra was out in the open, playing some energetic tunes to keep people moving. Jollity was returning, as were banter and larks. But Stanley knew the trouble was far from over.

'What was the beeping about?' he asked Rasmussen, as they stood amongst the crowd, drinking broth and digesting the goings-on of the last few hours.

'Not sure,' said Rasmussen. 'When a disembodied mechanical eye flies up in the air and emits a loud beeping sound, it could mean any one of a few different things. In this instance, I believe a signal of some sort was being emitted.'

'For whose benefit?' said Stanley. 'There's nobody for miles and miles all around!'

The Captain, sitting behind them, and apparently listening, butted in at this point.

'Zebediah,' he said quietly. 'He has a talent for creating machines and devices previously undreamt of. This . . . abomination . . .'

Here he indicated the remains of the mechanical man that were now lying at his feet.

'Is an invention of his, or of one of his devilish cohorts. That noise was a signal, sent over goodness knows how far, telling Zebediah everything that the machine-man had learned during his time on the Galloon.'

'Ah,' said Stanley, taking it all in.

'And so, as you have no doubt guessed, our work is far from done.'

The Captain stood up as he said this, and shrugged a thick blanket from his shoulders.

'Hurray!' said Rasmussen and Stanley together.

'Captain!' said a firm female voice beside them.

Ms Huntley, stepping through the crowd, had a determined look upon her face. She walked straight up to the Captain, and stood squarely in front of him, smaller but no less resolute than he.

'These are children,' she said firmly. 'Resourceful, clever, courageous children, no doubt, but children nonetheless. Please tell me that the things you are asking them – asking all of us – to do are of critical importance. We all feel for you and your lost love, but it would not be fair to ask the people of the Galloon to risk their lives only for your happiness.'

The Captain did not seem as astonished by this as perhaps he might, and Stanley had the feeling that this was a conversation they had had before, though probably not in quite such a public arena. Around them, though the party continued, Stanley was well aware of many listening ears, and he knew the Captain and Ms Huntley were too.

'I understand, Harissa, and I assure you – if assure is the right word – that this goes far beyond my own problems in love. The entire future of the Galloon is at stake. We must work together, for all our safety.'

Ms Huntley looked up at him, steeliness in her eyes, but no longer disapproving.

'Then tell us what we must do,' she said.

'Well, firstly, we must find out how Cloudier is doing . . .' said the Captain, in a concerned tone.

'Ah. I was hoping you had heard something I hadn't,' said Ms Huntley, clearly disappointed.

'No – I would tell you first. We haven't heard from her yet . . .' the Captain began again, before a voice interrupted from the crowd.

'Actually, we have,' said Clamdigger. He stepped forward, holding the rocket-shaped capsule in one hand, and a note in the other.

The Captain snatched the note from him, before remembering himself, and handing it to Ms Huntley. She read it in a second, and handed it to the Captain.

'She was well when this left her,' she said, her shoulders slumping with relief.

'A fine lookout!' said the Captain, almost to himself. Then he glanced at Ms Huntley and cleared his throat. 'We will make for her last-known location immediately, Harissa,' he said.

'Yes,' she said distractedly. 'I'll make the necessary calculations.'

With that, Ms Huntley stepped back through the dancing throng, on her way to the map room.

The Captain watched her go, and re-read the note. He appeared to make a decision, then turned to Rasmussen and Stanley.

'We,' he said conspiratorially, 'are going to see our old friend the Brunt!'

'Woohoo!' they cried, together.

* * *

Cloudier watched in amazement as a huge whale came to the surface just a few feet from where she crouched, peering over the edge of her little basket. It blew its hot breath high into the air, and glee bubbled up in her as she felt the spray on her face. The creature's long back slid past, then there was a moment before two huge tail flukes broke the surface, and the whale dived away.

At least she wasn't drifting too much – the ice in the bay seemed to be fairly static, and the Sumbaroon had stayed at least partly in view. She wasn't too worried about being discovered, as the night was still fairly dark, and unless they were actively looking for her, they were unlikely to notice the balloon against the backdrop of the foothills.

She watched now as the small figure she had seen clambering about atop Zebediah's vessel was joined by two others. Together, the three figures opened a hatch on the side of the Sumbaroon, and let out a long and murderous-looking harpoon. They swung it around expertly, following the movements of the great beast.

Cloudier was dismayed to see the whale rise again, well within range of the harpoon. She heard a faint cry of, 'Thar she blows!' on the wind, and saw one of the men swing the point of the weapon round.

'Surely they're not . . .' she said to herself, knowing full well that surely they were.

She let out an involuntary yelp, and stood up in her balloon as the Sumbarooners brought the harpoon to bear. Her heart was in her mouth when they turned, clearly having heard something that put them off their hunt.

Luckily, it took Cloudier only a moment to realise that the two men had in fact turned the other way – towards the conning tower of the Sumbaroon. Beside it, the long thin mast was clearly reacting to something unseen. A red light was flashing on and off at its very tip, intermittently, as if creating some sort of pattern. Cloudier didn't know what to make of it, but the Sumbarooners clearly did. Their shouts became cries of elation.

They scrambled to get the harpoon stowed away and as the first man went below, she worked out that the Sumbaroon was about to move off, and that she must make ready to follow it. The balloon above her head was still inflated, but only just enough to stop it flopping onto the ice – she'd have to spend a little while pumping hot air back into it, though she'd be grateful of the chance to warm up by the burner. Then there was the anchor – she glared down at it, and saw that it had become frozen into the ice.

'Oh, what's the point? It's all hopeless! Hopeless, I say!' she said for the look of the thing, but she was over the edge of the basket in a moment and tugging at the anchor for all she was worth.

Glancing up, she saw that the Sumbarooners had clambered out of their hatch again, and were dismantling the tall aerial into shorter sections, which they fed down the hatch to unseen hands. This done, they went back below, and the periscope poking from the top of the vessel began to look around for the first time. The waters around the underwater boat began to churn and boil, and the Sumbaroon moved slowly forward, out of the lee of the hat-shaped rock.

Still Cloudier tugged at the anchor, with a rising sense of panic. It was firmly lodged. The initial impact of throwing it down had cracked the top layers of ice, which had then refrozen as she staked out the Sumbaroon. Now it might as well have been welded in. Her fingerless gloves gave little protection as she grappled with the painfully cold metal. To make matters worse, as she glanced up again, she realised that the Sumbaroon was heading directly towards her.

A coincidence, surely? she thought as she continued to try and free the anchor. But no, the Sumbaroon had come round in an arc, and was now heading straight at her. Anyone using that periscope must surely have seen her little balloon by now. Frantically she started to kick at the anchor, but it was useless. The Sumbaroon was picking up speed, and in the starlight she saw its front end rise slightly from the water like a shark's nose.

Cloudier suddenly felt utterly exposed. She took a look around, in case this was the last view she ever saw before being pitched into the soupy, icy water. The hills loomed behind, and the white crests of the waves were breaking on the nearby shore. The ice all around seemed to be heaving a little more now than before, and in the starlight she felt for a moment like she was standing on a gigantic bedspread, each ice floe a square in some frost-giant's quilt.

But she snapped back to herself, and spotted something new. Another plume of vapour, off to the left, but surely heading for the Sumbaroon? The craft was almost upon her now, and Cloudier saw that the intention of its evil master must have been to crash straight through her little ice-island, pitching her and her balloon into the water, or worse. She had often wondered what poetic thoughts she would come up with in this direst of moments, but was not surprised when an image of the Galloon's hot little mess room came into her mind. She was surprised, however, when the stripy-jumpered boy in the daydream opened his mouth, and made a noise like a cockerel swallowing a banshee. She jumped as the hooked beak of Fishbane the Wanderer flashed past her nose, almost into the water, but caught her balance and watched as Fishbane landed on the edge of her basket again, and squirted a long line of hot fishy poo out of his feathery bottom.

139

'Oh, this is really not the time . . .' said Cloudier instinctively, before realising that this was, in fact, just the time. A more timely poo she could not imagine, as the stinky substance landed on the anchor, and began to fizz and bubble where it met the ice. Fishbane pooed again, with feeling, and squawked his inimitable squawk. Against all her better judgement, Cloudier put her hands round the anchor chain, and resumed pulling. There was definitely more give this time, as the astringent poop began to melt the ice around the anchor. She was grateful to see that Fishbane, while pooing usefully out of one end, was using his formidable beak at the other to turn on the gas burner. This would allow them to take off quickly, if they could get the anchor free before the Sumbaroon hit.

The metal beast was now only about a hundred feet away, and Cloudier could see that its sheet-iron nose was even painted in the likeness of a shark's mouth. She closed her eyes, and yanked once more on the anchor chain. It was almost free, but there was no time! Without opening her eyes, she waited for the crash that would inevitably come. Beside her, Fishbane took off, and she could not blame him – she only hoped he would tell her mother what had happened.

'CRUNCH!'

Came the noise that Cloudier had been braced for,

and along with it a soaking, freezing wave of slushy water. Cloudier's breath was taken from her, but somehow she was still standing. Still clutching the anchor chain, she managed to open one eye.

Ahead of her, the Sumbaroon had, for some reason, come to a dead stop a mere twenty feet away. The soaking had come from its bow-wave washing over the little floe. Chattering and gibbering from the cold, Cloudier looked on in awe as a leviathan, a whale almost the length of the Sumbaroon itself, rose from the waves off to one side, and plumed impressively. It was gone for a moment, and then it leapt from the water and breached, a huge, warty, barnacle-crusted leap of triumph, before crashing back down with an immense thump and splash. The sound slapped into Cloudier's ears like an insult, and her mind boggled as she tried to take in what had occurred.

The Sumbaroon had rolled over a few degrees, and she could see that one side of it was dented and smashed, the iron panels buckled and torn. Piecing things together, she realised that the huge whale must have rammed the Sumbaroon, perhaps in anger at the presence of the harpoon, perhaps at some word from Fishbane, perhaps in revenge at some historic wrong. Who could say? But she had been saved.

Fishbane landed again on the balloon, and Cloudier found that she was now holding the anchor, freed from its mooring, in her hands. She hoiked it aboard, and clambered over the edge as Fishbane let yet more hot air into the envelope. Her feeling of joy as she felt the little basket lift from the ice was only marred by her realisation that the Sumbaroon was not entirely defunct. She heard its engines sputter back into life and saw the water around it turn white once more. As she rose into the air, she was amazed to see the hatch open again, and a head and shoulders pop out.

The Captain himself! But how . . .? No – of course, this was Zebediah, the author of all their recent troubles. Wearing the Captain's best hat, a gold-piped model even more impressive than the one his brother habitually wore about the Galloon, Zebediah clambered out and stood on the hull of the Sumbaroon.

'You have been saved, girl!' he called, in a voice that barely carried over the wind and the crashing of the sea. 'I would have crushed you! Tell your master that I know – I know about the pendant! I know it lies in the Kraken's Lair, and I know how to use it against him! And as soon as I have repaired my ship, I will be there, while he is still entertaining the inbreeds and ingrates of Castle Eisberg! His bride will be mine forever, and soon his Galloon will follow! Ahahahaha! Mwahahaha! MWWWAAAAAAHHHAAAAAHHHAAAA!'

At this, Cloudier heard another voice, sweeter and clearer in the night air, emerge from the hatchway.

'Who are you talking to, dearest?'

'Just, erm . . . assessing the damage, my darling!' called Zebediah, in a much deeper voice than before. 'We must have hit an iceberg. Soon be dealt with, and we'll be on our way again!'

Cloudier was now almost out of earshot, but she saw the Captain's evil brother walking back along the Sumbaroon, heedless of the icy depths to each side, to see what damage the vengeful whale had done.

'He may be completely barmy,' she said aloud. 'But he's brave enough in his way.'

'SKWAAAAWWWWWWWWWWW-AK-AK-AK-AK-AKEEEEEEEEEEEEEEEEEEEE!!!!!' agreed Fishbane at her side.

'The Kraken's Lair!' said Cloudier, warming her soaking self at the burner once more. 'So that's where Isabella's half of the pendant is. If he gets that, he'll be halfway to taking control of the Galloon! We must get there, but how will we ever find it?'

With a croak that may have been the Seagle's version of a resigned roll of the eyes, Fishbane began to peck and claw at one of the many thin cords that held the balloon in a protective web.

'Ermm . . . please don't . . .' said Cloudier, but she stopped as Fishbane gave her one of his looks.

He must know what he's doing, she thought, and so it proved.

144

Once Fishbane had a longish cord loose, he took it in his beak, and gave Cloudier a baleful look that she took to mean, 'I don't do this for just anyone, you know'. That done, he turned the burner off to stop the balloon rising any further, and dropped from the edge of the basket into thin air. He soon rose again into Cloudier's eye line, with the cord clamped tightly in his serrated beak. His huge wings flapping slowly, he began to pull the balloon round, so that the wind was once more at their backs. And in this way, with the Lord of the Wandering Seagles towing her through the sky, and with the recent perils apparently behind her at least for the moment, Cloudier sat back to enjoy the ride to the Kraken's Lair.

'I would die, Captain Meredith,' said the Brunt, matter-of-factly. 'I cannot go out into the snow. I would die.'

The Captain winced slightly at this reminder of the Brunt's mortality, but he was not to be put off.

'But if we could find a way to keep you warm, my friend? You'd do it? For the Galloon?'

The Captain took a lump of sugar from a smartly dressed mouse with barely a blink.

'I don't like going outside, Captain Meredith,' said the Brunt, appearing to think very carefully as he stared at the ceiling of his hot little room, down in the bowels of the Galloon where people rarely went. 'But I would like to see the inside of a firehill again.'

'Firehill?' said Rasmussen, who was busy tying her last ribbon round another mouse, who had been trained by the Brunt to dance the galliard.

'Volcano,' said the Captain, his urgency fairly thrumming through him, despite his being sat in a chintzy chair, drinking tea from a cracked china cup. 'The Brunt was born in one, many years since. It is his natural home.'

'This is my natural home now, Rasmussen,' said the Brunt, firmly but quietly.

'Of course, of course it is, my old friend,' said the Captain, leaning in towards the huge creature, whose impressive horns curled so high they nearly hit the ceiling of the room, even when he was sitting down.

'And if it wasn't in danger, we wouldn't be here, except perhaps for tea and cake. But if Zebediah gets to the firehill first, he will have won. And I have no doubt that, so emboldened, he will keep making attempts on the Galloon itself, until it is his, or destroyed.'

Stanley and Rasmussen knew that when standing up, the Brunt had to stoop slightly to fit in here, even though it was his bedroom, living room, and, for all

146

they knew, his kitchen and bathroom too. It wasn't that there wasn't more space for him – he just didn't seem to want it. Stanley and Rasmussen had become fairly regular visitors since they stumbled upon the Brunt's little room during a previous adventure, and they had become firm friends with him. Despite their love for the Captain, there was something unsettling for Stanley in seeing the Brunt put under this pressure. He almost seemed to squirm in his chair as conflicting expressions flowed across his huge, deeply lined face.

'I like living here, Captain Meredith,' he said simply.

'And we like you living here!' said the Captain. 'But if I don't get my hands on the token of love I made for my Isabella, then the very future of the Galloon is at stake.'

'I think I have an idea as to how we can keep you safe from the cold,' said Rasmussen, but Stanley wasn't sure anyone else had heard her.

The cup in the Captain's hand cracked like an eggshell, and Stanley felt the force of his feeling, but he also knew how much the idea of going outside scared the Brunt. This could go either way.

The Brunt's brow furrowed yet further, and he turned to look straight into the Captain's eyes.

'Do you love her, Captain Meredith?' he said.

'Of course! Well . . . yes! I mean . . . What kind

of . . .? Yes! Hang it all, Brunt, what d'yer . . .?' stammered the Captain, and Stanley found this most unsettling of all. Beside him, Rasmussen stopped playing with the mouse, and watched the Captain carefully.

'Then I will go,' said the Brunt.

The Captain, still a tad flustered, looked again at the Brunt, and Stanley thought he saw a tear in his eye.

'I wouldn't ask you if I didn't love her. She's my home,' he said.

'I meant Isabella, not the Galloon, Captain Meredith.'

The Captain squeezed his eyes tight shut for a moment, then looked up at the Brunt.

'So did I.'

For the first time, Stanley thought about the power of these two people, and he realised that the Brunt, quiet though he was, was not some underling here. He was every bit the Captain's equal. To Stanley's surprise, the Brunt nodded briefly at the Captain but then turned to Rasmussen and Stanley before he spoke again.

'Tell me your idea, please, Rasmussen,' he said.

Rasmussen jumped from her chair, and clapped her hands decisively.

'I'll do better than that,' she said. 'I'll show you!'

*   *   *

148

Flying through the air behind Fishbane, the Lord of Three of the Four Winds, Cloudier finally had time to update her journal.

I do not think it will take Zebediah's men long to repair the Sumbaroon, and then they will be heading straight for the Kraken's Lair. We will get there before them, however, and I must use whatever time advantage I have to find that token!

She looked up from her writing, to where Fishbane was still flying ahead, dragging her small balloon through the skies.

Was the whale a stroke of luck? Or did Fishbane have something to do with it? Perhaps he is not just the Lord of the Seagles, but of all creatures. Or perhaps all Seagles refer to themselves as Lords, and he's just like all the others. I will ask him one day – but I'll put a cagoule on first.

As she wrote this, she feared she had been found out, because Fishbane let out a skreeeek. But when she looked up, she realised that he was indicating that they were starting to lose height. Cloudier stood and peered through the moonlit night. She could see the ice, reflecting moonlight up into the sky, so she knew they were still over the water, but ahead of them were patches of darkness. Islands perhaps, or mountains emerging from the sea? Fishbane seemed to be heading for one off to their left slightly. As her eyes got used to the distance, she could see that this was a large island, consisting almost entirely of one great volcano, which seemed to have a plume of smoke emerging from its open top. Down by sea level, she thought she could see occasional flashes of orange light, which made no sense to her for quite a while.

They continued their approach, and it seemed to Cloudier that Fishbane was flying faster now their destination was in sight. For this was surely the Kraken's Lair, scene of that disastrous day a year or two before, when the Captain had forged a love token for Isabella, given half to her on a beautiful golden necklace, but then dropped his half down into the crater.

Now, as well as orange flashes, she could hear, over the wind of their progress, occasional hisses, as of something hot being plunged into water. She wished she could ask Fishbane what was going on, but as he was busy tugging the balloon, and could only communicate with her in writing at the best of times, she would have to work it out for herself. So – a volcano, in the sea, with orange flashes and hissing noises.

Staring intently, she could see that the orange light was coming from a point where the volcano met the water, and where there seemed to be a darker patch. A cave perhaps?

This was confirmed as they drew closer, and she began to make out puffs of steam coming from the cave, as well as the smoke pouring from the open mountaintop. They were now level with this, thanks to Fishbane's hard work. He dropped the rope he had been holding, and Cloudier gave the balloon a burst from the burner to keep it at the right level. Fishbane flew on ahead, as she continued more slowly on her way, by virtue of the prevailing winds.

She watched as Fishbane flew directly over the volcano for a second, before wheeling away, perhaps repelled by the smoke and heat. He flew back to her, and perched on the edge of the basket. Unsure what to do, Cloudier emptied some heat from the balloon, which caused it to sink, and seemed to please the Seagle. Soon they were floating slowly down towards the sea, and the winds were not so strong down here. Through a combination of Cloudier managing the balloon, and Fishbane giving the occasional tug on the lead rope, they were heading towards the dark patch – now clearly a large sea cave where the mountain met the water, and just as clearly, the place where Fishbane thought they should be.

Soon they were skimming dangerously low over the crests of the waves, with only occasional bursts from the burner keeping them from plunging into the sea. Cloudier's heart leapt to her mouth again, as she realised that they had more chance of tipping into the water, or slamming into the side of the mountain, than they did of navigating directly into the upcoming cave mouth, and even if they made it inside, she would then be piloting a hot air balloon *inside an active volcano*.

For the first time, she felt the full weight of responsibility. There was a great deal at stake. If Zebediah found the token first, then . . .

Then what? The Captain had indicated that the Galloon's future was at stake here. But how was anybody's guess. She would just have to trust that the mission he had sent her out on was an important one. There was no more time for this train of thought – the volcano was looming, and if she missed the yawning cave mouth, she would be dashed to pieces on the dark mountainside.

Up ahead, Fishbane had hold of the rope again, and was using it to make fine adjustments to their flight path. The orange flashes were brighter now and seemed more frequent, each one accompanied by a hiss and a burst of steam. Her stomach flipped as the entrance to the cave flashed by, and then suddenly they were inside.

With almost no time to be relieved, she saw ahead of them the reason for the flashes. From a yawning gulf in the cave wall, many yards ahead, rivers of lava were flowing. The orange-hot, gloopy-looking stuff was pouring over onto a wide shelf of rock, where it pooled and spread into a lake of fire, dotted with occasional outcrops and islands. Every once in a while, the lava overflowed from this lake, and huge gobs of it plopped into the sea, which was lapping and crashing against the near edge of the shelf. Each time it did this, a huge cloud of steam burst from the water. She could see, through the waves, that the magma fell away through the water as it cooled, and some of it was still bright orange as it dropped from sight into the unknown depths of the sea.

Despite the chill water and the open cave mouth, the heat inside the cavern was intense. The little balloon had begun to rise on the column of hot air, and Fishbane let go of the rope, as it was yanked and buffeted about by the thermals. Cloudier grabbed onto the basket and held on tight. She was amazed to glimpse the stars through the opening at the top of the volcano. If she hadn't been in mortal danger she would have laughed with joy at the silliness of it all – but the walls of the cave were closing in as she rose, and she now had almost no control over the balloon's progress. The smoke was enveloping her, and she was in danger of choking, or being smashed against the rock walls, or dropping out of the balloon and either drowning or burning up in the maelstrom below.

She heard Fishbane's squawk above the rush of the water and steam, and hoped that he was okay. The balloon seemed to be sticking now, either caught on an outcrop or pressed against the inward slope of the wall. Either way, it was no longer climbing, and it was, at least for a while, out of the main rush of smoke heading towards the chimney. Cloudier looked around, hoping to see Fishbane nearby, but he was not there. She peered down towards the base of the cave, where the fiery lake was still being filled up, and then over-flowing with a hiss. If the Captain's love token had fallen into the lava, or into the chill waters of the Great Northern Ocean, it was surely lost forever? Even if it had landed on one of the outcrops of solid rock dotted here and there about the lava lake, the chances of getting it back were miniscule.

Just as she thought she could not feel any more hopeless, her spirits plummeted yet further. As she peered through the gloom and the heat haze towards the cave mouth, she saw a sight to freeze her blood. There, chugging its way slowly into the cave, was the battered Sumbaroon. Cloudier watched as it gingerly picked its way past the rocks at the entrance to this hellish place.

'He must have followed us!' she said to herself, and then jumped almost out of her skin as the Seagle, who had landed on the basket behind her, let fly an ear-splitting screech.

She turned to admonish him, but soon realised that he had an urgent request. He hopped down into the basket, in which there was barely room for them both, and picked up Cloudier's damp and crinkly note-book. She opened it for him, and handed him a pen, which he took with rather less care than he could have, leaving Cloudier with a nipped finger.

The Seagle's head dipped and swooped, and Cloudier tried to read over his shoulder as he wrote. She could make no sense of it, until he dropped the pen, picked up the notebook and held it out for her to read.

We have two hopes – Water and air. I will find the Kraken, the denizen of this lair, and warn him of the Sumbaroon's proximity. He will relish a chance to finish the job he has started. I will then make for the Galloon to warn them of your plight. Stay here, stay alive, and keep an eye on the Sumbaroon. Look for salvation when the darkness deepens.

Fishbane, Who Flies Into Fire.

And with that, he was gone.

'Look for salvation when the darkness deepens?' sneered Cloudier, despite herself. 'Such hyperbole!'

In the main kitchen of the Great Galloon, the Brunt was being made cold-proof. As well as his traditional leather apron and greasy trousers, he was now wearing a kind of all-over quilted body suit, which Stanley had remembered seeing the last time they had visited the Brunt's hot little rooms. It turned out that the Brunt used it to protect himself on those rare occasions when he had to actually step into the Galloon's great furnace, to clean it or make repairs.

He was standing by the huge range cooker, yet still he was shivering in the relative cool of the kitchen. Stanley and Rasmussen were wrapping blankets and towels round his arms and legs, while the Captain and Cook were busy shovelling hot coals from the range into a series of bedpans, kettles and casserole dishes. Any metal receptacle with a lid had been pressed into service. Once every exposed area of fur or flesh had been covered, they began to hang these hot pots from his neck, sling them across his back with ropes, and generally ensure that as much of his body as possible was covered with heating pans.

His feet, also wrapped in damp cloths to prevent the fur singeing, were stuffed into great fish kettles full of embers, and his hands thrust into the biggest oven gloves they could find, and again stuffed with ash and cinders from the range. Finally they tied a bag full of hot stones, warmed in the oven, round his head like a hat. All this would have been enough to kill any other member of the crew. But Stanley noticed that the Brunt became more relaxed with every garment added, until eventually he was beaming beatifically and almost purring with delight.

'This is very comfortable, thank you, Stanley,' said the Brunt.

'You're welcome,' said Stanley.

'Thank you, Rasmussen,' said the Brunt.

'You're welcome,' said Rasmussen.

'Thank you, Cook,' said the Brunt.

'You're welcome,' said Cook.

'Thank you, Captain Meredith,' said the Brunt.

'You're welcome,' said the Captain.

Stanley, for one, was pleased no one else had helped. 'That should keep you warm in almost any conditions,' he said.

'For a time at least,' added the Captain. 'Though we will be up against it. Once you are inside the volcano, and you've found the token, you can refill the suit with hot rocks and head back out.'

'Yes, Captain Meredith.'

'Can you move?' asked Rasmussen.

'Yes, Rasmussen,' said the Brunt, and he walked round in a little circle to show them. He could indeed move comfortably, although woe betide anyone who stood nearby as a cloud of hot ash and cinders blew up about him as he went.

'Then let us head out on deck – we've been travelling at full sail for some time now, and I think with these following winds, we should be able to see the Chimney Isles approaching.'

And indeed they could – a short while later, as Stanley, Rasmussen, the Brunt and Captain Anstruther stood at the prow of the ship, they could see jagged mountain peaks reaching up from the icy waters. The Captain must have given orders for the Galloon to lose height, as it was closer now to the water than Stanley could ever remember it being, and it looked to him as if some of those mountain peaks would loom over them if they got much closer. From each volcanic island, a column of smoke rose high in the air before dissipating in the strong winds.

From far behind them, the sound of revelry could be heard, as the Grand Winter Ball was still in full swing. Party-goers were now spread out around the decks of the Great Galloon, and their arrival had given one young couple the fright of their lives, as they lay out on Claude's head, looking up at the stars.

'The Chimney Isles!' said Stanley, and beside him the Captain grunted agreement.

'Yes, lad. And there, dead ahead, is the one known as "Kraken's Lair". We'll be there before long.'

'Why is it called . . .?' Rasmussen began to ask, but her question was interrupted by a deathly scream, which would have given them the screaming heebie-jeebies if they hadn't met Fishbane before. He swooped in and landed clumsily on the taffrail ahead of them, which was the final straw for the young couple. They clambered over the rail, apologising as they went, and disappeared back towards the party. Not a moment too soon, as Fishbane let go with his trademark long white squirt of poo just where they had been lying.

'Fishbane!' cried the Captain, with genuine delight. 'What news? Have you seen it? Have you found the token? Seen my dastardly brother? Tell all!'

'And how is Cloudier?' asked Rasmussen, at which the Captain jumped visibly.

'Egad! Of course! How's the young lookout? Keeping out of danger, I hope?' he cried.

At this, the Seagle, unable to make himself understood any other way, shook his head frantically.

'Not out of danger? *In* danger?' snapped the Captain.

The Seagle nodded and pointed a wing towards the Kraken's Lair.

'You don't mean . . .?' yelped Stanley.

Fishbane nodded.

'You can't mean . . .?' cried Rasmussen.

Fishbane nodded.

'You wouldn't mean . . .?' roared the Captain.

Fishbane nodded.

'What do you mean, large bird?' said the Brunt.

'Cloudier is in the Kraken's Lair – and she's in danger!' yelled Stanley and Rasmussen together.

'What have I done?' said the Captain, and he swung round, so that he was facing the three of them.

'Stanley, Rasmussen, find Clamdigger. Ask him to prepare the boatswain's chair for the Brunt's descent. If we can get you in there, Brunt, perhaps you can protect her. Fishbane, hurry to her and do all you can. I will go and find Harissa Huntley. By all that's good in the world, may nothing happen to that child. Go!' he cried.

Everybody jumped to action – Fishbane leapt from the rail and soared away, Stanley and Rasmussen ran off to find Clamdigger, and Captain Anstruther and the Brunt lumbered away to look for Ms Huntley.

'I hope everything will be okay!' said Stanley as they went.

'Of course it will! This is the Captain we're talking about!' said Rasmussen.

But, for the first time in a long while, Stanley wasn't so sure.

GOODNIGHT!

Cloudier was running out of poems. It was a habit with her to recite poetry to herself in times of great peril, but until a couple of months ago the greatest peril she had ever been in was being embarrassed at a party. In the last couple of months she had been attacked by monster moths while dangling in mid-air from a rope with no safety net, flown over icy seas in pursuit of a known kidnapper, come within feet of being squished by a Sumbaroon, almost frozen to death on a precarious ice floe, and now she was sitting on a rock ledge halfway down an active volcano, watching the Captain's brother go about his nefarious business.

Far below her, little figures were standing on the Sumbaroon, scouring the volcano with telescopes, binoculars and similar equipment. Her balloon was wedged against the inside of the volcano, like the ones you find on the ceiling three days after a birthday party. She had not been seen yet, as the Sumbarooners' focus was looking for the love token, but perhaps it was only a matter of time. She was trying to work out how to dislodge the balloon, and whether she could make it out of the top of the volcano, when something extraordinary happened.

Far below her, she heard a blast of air, and then an almighty splash. The water near the Sumbaroon was a maelstrom of white foam, and as she looked a pair of gigantic tail flukes broke the surface once again. The whale had returned! It clearly had revenge on its mind, as it began circling the Sumbaroon, smashing its great tail against the water, making all the Sumbarooners on top of the vessel rush for the hatches.

'Hurrah!' cried Cloudier to no one in particular, pleased to have found another ally.

Immediately though, her attention was drawn to what was happening above her. When the smoke occasionally cleared, she knew it was now a bright moonlit night. She had glimpses of the stars, and some of their light was infiltrating the cavern. But suddenly the stars blinked out completely. The quality of the light in the volcano changed, as now the only source was the orange and red of the lava. Cloudier felt a surge of hope. It wasn't the smoke that was causing this blackout, as that seemed, if anything, less thick than before. Cloudier could only think of one thing capable of blocking out the starlight over a volcano. She dared to hope that the Galloon had come for her.

'Look for salvation when the darkness deepens.'

She craned her neck, and saw the Sumbarooners below, some now spreading out in a variety of small boats. A few were taking on the whale, which was still circling and smashing its great tail into the water, and she was pleased to see that so far no one had any chance to start looking for the necklace.

Looking up, she could see nothing at the mouth of the volcano for a while, until her eyes grew accustomed to the darkness. She squinted a little, convinced she had seen some movement through the smoke. Surely that was a person? But too big, even to be the Captain. Was she mistaken, was it possible that this was not the Galloon at all, but some hideous contrivance of Zebediah's?

The figure was getting closer now, and she could make out a cloud around it. A cloud of dust, or ash, which made no sense. Down below, she could hear the Sumbarooners shouting to each other, and she thought she detected a change in tone – had they noticed this newcomer too?

Her heart swelled as the big figure was lowered through the heat haze, past the worst of the smoke, and into focus. It was the Brunt! She had been to visit him a couple of times with Stanley and Rasmussen, and knew that he was immensely kind and strong, but as far as she knew he had never been outside the

Galloon in all the time she had been onboard. There was no time for questions, however, as he was getting closer. She could hear the pots and pans clanging about him as he came, and soon he was within earshot.

'Hello, Cloudier Peele!' he called, waving a gloved hand.

'Hello, the Brunt!' cried Cloudier, happier to see him than she had ever been to see anyone before.

'I will take you home now,' said the Brunt, as he came alongside, and gave two strong tugs on the rope.

'But . . . but . . . how are you here?' she managed to say. 'The cold . . . how can you?'

'Stanley and Rasmussen made me a Stay-Hot Suit!' He grinned. 'Be careful!'

Saying this, he reached out and plucked Cloudier from her basket as if she were no heavier than an egg, and held her at arm's length, so that she wouldn't touch any of the scalding-hot metal about his person. Immediately, despite being dangled in the air hundreds of feet above a lake of molten lava, Cloudier felt safer than she had felt in days. The Brunt tugged twice more on the rope, and they began to ascend.

'Wait!' shouted Cloudier. 'What about the love token? He needs it to keep the Galloon safe!'

'The Captain says, "Bring back Cloudier. Forget necklace," Cloudier.'

'But . . . his bride . . . the Galloon . . .' stuttered

164

Cloudier, as they ascended jerkily through the huge space.

Far below, Cloudier's attention was drawn by a loud crack and a crunch. She looked down, and saw that the whale had rammed the Sumbaroon once again, and had indeed finished the job it started. The great iron vessel was bent like a banana, and many of the crew were making off in their small boats as best they could. Cloudier saw the whale dive, and as it didn't come up, she thought its onslaught must be over.

To her astonishment, two figures remained on top of the Sumbaroon – one in a large black hat, clinging to a willowy figure in a long white dress. Could it be Captain Zebediah and Isabella? As Cloudier gaped, they seemed to look up and point.

'I think they've seen us!' gasped Cloudier.

The Brunt gave another tug on the wrist-thick rope that was keeping them up in the sky, and they began to move more quickly. Cloudier imagined Clamdigger turning the hefty winch, but knew that with the Brunt's immense weight, there must have been a team of strong crewmembers helping him.

'Look up!' said the Brunt, in his simple way. So Cloudier did.

There, hanging on an outcrop of rock at the very lip of the crater, where the cold night air met the column of smoke and soot, something gleamed. They were being winched towards it, inch by inch, and Cloudier scarcely dared to believe that it was what it appeared to be, even when they drew level with it.

Hanging on a little jagged edge of rock, where the Captain had accidentally dropped it many moons before, was the lost love token of Captain Meredith Anstruther. It was a simple task for Cloudier to reach out, grab it, and wrap it twice round her wrist.

'Ha ha!' she laughed, showing the beautiful thing to the Brunt. 'We found it!'

'Yes, Cloudier,' said the Brunt, but the look on his face told her he was as elated as she was. Catching her eye again, the Brunt jerked his head skywards.

Cloudier's breath left her as she took in the immensity of the Galloon, hanging in the sky over the Kraken's Lair. The keel of the thing, encrusted with cloud barnacles like sharp little mountains in themselves, was only a few dozen feet away, but that meant they were still hundreds of feet below the level of the main deck, where Clamdigger was toiling to bring them onboard. Far off in front, Cloudier could make out Claude's enormous feet, and way astern, the system of rudders and ailerons that allowed the Galloon to be steered through the sky. In between just a huge, bulbous expanse, like the underside of the whale, only hundreds of times as huge.

The Brunt, still holding Cloudier at arm's length, to keep her safe from his heat pans, began to look worried as the cold night air hit.

'We'll soon be back onboard, and we'll be heroes!' called Cloudier. 'Then you can get straight back down to the furnace to warm up.'

'Yes, Cloudier,' said the Brunt, as the juddering rope brought them up through the mouth of the volcano for the first time, and out into the great crater at its peak. Snow lay on the ground, even this close to the blistering heat below.

Cloudier knew that keeping the Galloon so steady must have been nigh on impossible, and she was not surprised to see that, now they were clear, the great ship began to drift slightly, so that as well as being pulled up through the sky, they were floating now across the snowy, rocky landscape. It would have been beautiful if it weren't so terrifying, and she just wished they were safely back onboard.

But these thoughts were interrupted by a stinging slap on the side of her face. Then another jolt, as something cold and wet hit her in the back. She twisted round, and to her horror saw a detachment of Sumbarooners, who had been left up here as lookouts, throwing snowballs at them as they dangled helplessly. She looked at the Brunt, just as a snowball hit him smack in the eye, and another clanged against a casserole dish full of cinders, and turned to slush with a hiss.

'Cold!' cried the Brunt, in genuine distress, and Cloudier was mortified to feel his grip slacken around her. More snowballs hit her, and she could see that there was now quite a gathering of Sumbarooners on the lip of the crater.

Still they were rising, but it seemed to Cloudier that something was wrong – perhaps the mechanism was not strong enough to carry both of them, or perhaps there wasn't room for enough people to help with the winching. They seemed to be slowing down just as they needed to get out of trouble. Snowballs were landing thick and fast now, and while it was irritating for Cloudier, it could be deadly for the Brunt.

A big sloppy snowball hit him square in the face, and another landed on his neck and went down his collar. Some of his metal warming pans were now covered in snowballs, and rather than melt straight off, they were beginning to stick. Looking down, Cloudier saw to her dismay that they were moving closer to the crowd of Sumbarooners on the crater's edge, and that there were now a couple of dozen men and women there, with more arriving all the time. One seemed to be wielding a long boathook, and they would soon be in range of it. Cloudier winced as more snowballs hit, and she knew this was no coincidence – the Sumbarooners knew just how dangerous this could be for the Brunt.

'Cold, Cloudier . . .' said the Brunt, and she saw that his head-warmer had been knocked clean off by the torrent of snowballs.

'Come on, Clamdigger!' said Cloudier through gritted teeth, but as she did so, the rope stopped, then let them down a few feet. Still being held at arm's length, Cloudier felt the Brunt's grip begin to fail.

'No! The Brunt! Think warm thoughts!' she called, but to her horror they were now within range of the boathook-wielding Sumbarooner. He was standing on the shoulders of another man, and as Cloudier kicked and tried to twist away, he managed to get a purchase on one of the Brunt's big fish-kettle footwarmers. He yanked and tugged, and there was nothing Cloudier could do to stop him pulling the outsize shoe off and throwing it down into the snow. The Brunt looked terrified as the boathook wielder got hold of his other foot, and began to denude that too.

'Hold on, Cloudier!' he cried, as he lifted her into a position from where she could hold onto the rope herself, rather than rely on his grip. He began to kick out with his feet, but the Sumbarooners were wily enough to stay out of the way, while still pelting him with snowballs.

Cloudier cried out as the boathook man got hold of

the ropes tying pans and pots to the Brunt's left leg, and began to pull for all he was worth. Soon three Sumbarooners were clinging to him, and the Brunt was slipping dangerously out of the boatswain's chair. His immense strength would be no match for any three humans in normal circumstances, but now he was caked in snowballs, and clearly suffering with the cold. With enormous presence of mind, he ripped a huge pan from his chest and poured the hot coals down on their assailants, but they managed to avoid injury, and this left the Brunt with even less heat protection.

'Slipping, Cloudier,' he said, and Cloudier saw that he was indeed close to falling out completely, with the three Sumbarooners hanging onto his leg.

'I won't . . . let you . . . go . . .' grunted Cloudier, now hanging onto the rope with one hand, while clinging to the Brunt's apron with the other. But it was useless – his great weight was now tipping slowly from the harness, and she was distressed to see his eyes begin to roll back in his head, as more and more snowballs hit the exposed areas of fur.

As in a dream, Cloudier felt the Brunt slip from the boatswain's chair, just as his eyes closed. Barely conscious now, he tumbled the ten or twelve feet to the floor of the crater, where he landed with an almighty thump in a pile of snow, the Sumbarooners around him whooping their victory.

'Nooooo!' yelled Cloudier, and then distress turned to despair when she looked at her wrist, where the love token had been. It was no longer there. It must have got caught on the Brunt's apron strings, and was now lying next to him in the snow. The Sumbarooners didn't look like they had noticed it yet, but they soon would, and it would all have been in vain.

Clinging to the rope, which was moving much more quickly now, Cloudier wept. The figure of the Brunt, lying almost senseless in the snow, was still enormous and imposing as it receded, but as the Sumbarooners closed round it, all seemed lost.

On the deck, Clamdigger, Stanley, Tarheel and Tamp were now manning the winch, but it was slow work. The Brunt had gone over the side, no problem, and they had managed to navigate him into the mouth of the volcano, but after that it had been guesswork, as the Captain stood up on the quarterdeck with Ms Huntley, yelling out occasional orders and trying to keep the Galloon as still as possible, and the winch team did their best to interpret what was going on at the end of the rope. Around them, most of the partygoers were now gathered in a respectful if, in parts, slightly sozzled crowd.

'Try winding that winch roun' and roun',' said a rotund man at the front of the crowd, not put off by the fact that that was exactly what they had been doing for the past twenty minutes.

'What was that?' said Clamdigger to the Countess, who was standing nearby, leaning over the rail.

'I've no idea, Jack – did it feel like two tugs?' she said.

'No,' said Stanley. 'It felt like an extra weight on the rope.'

'And now,' Clamdigger said, looking with concern at the rest of the winch team, 'and now, it feels extremely light.'

'My word. Could the rope have snapped?' said the Countess.

'No – something's still on it. I fear something's going wrong down there, I really do!' said Clamdigger, desperately heaving on the winch.

'Oh my. If only there was some way of seeing what was going on,' said the Countess, putting a hand to her mouth.

'Ermmm,' said Rasmussen, who was sitting in the rigging by the Countess's head. 'There is!'

172

'What? What do you mean, darling?' said the Countess.

'What about all these magnificent toffs and their flying machines?' said Stanley, pointing to the charabanc that Charlie had flown aboard earlier that day, though it felt like a lifetime ago.

'Why . . . of course,' said the Countess. And then, turning to the crowd of assembled partygoers and Gallooniers, 'My friends, would you . . .?'

'Rather!' came the reply, and ''course we would!' and 'Tally pip and toodle-ho!' and 'Where d'you want us?' and any number of other affirmative variations, as the partygoers who had arrived by flying machine scrambled to their places, and lined up for take-off, lift-off, bunk-up, and all the other methods they employed to get off the ground.

A symphony of growls, rumbles, flaps and whirs accompanied the starting up of the flying machines, and Stanley for one was extremely pleased when Hawthorne, the Count of Eisberg's trusty guard, called to him and Rasmussen.

'Hop in, Stanley!' he called, as he sat in the front seat of the winged omnibus. 'Rasmussen, you too – you don't want to miss the action!'

So they hopped up into the long bench seat next to Hawthorne, and pulled the seat belt across both of them at once. And not a moment too soon – next to

173

them, the gyrocopter spluttered and chuffed into the air, a flimsy-looking biplane shot past them across the decks, and the balloon-type craft, its bellows being pumped by a grumbling Mr Wouldbegood, popped and farted its way off the deck.

Hawthorne backed the steam-driven beast up a little, then threw a long lever that stuck up between his legs. There was a moment of stillness, during which a number of ball guests clambered into the back of the omnibus, and the machine began to trundle across the deck towards the rail.

'Woopwoopwoop!!!' cried Rasmussen, as they careered across the Galloon, scattering ball-goers and Gallooniers as they went.

'Go get 'em, fellas!' called Clamdigger, as the chara-banc's canvas wings gained just enough lift to take it off the deck, and over the taffrail. Stanley's stomach flipped as the scene below them became a snowy slope, hundreds of feet beneath, upon which he could just make out crowds of Sumbarooners converging on a point in the shadow of the Great Galloon.

Fishbane screamed past them, squawking at the top of his lungs, and Stanley felt a thrill as he watched the Seagle drop into a steep dive, aiming his stoop at a cluster of Sumbarooners.

'Look behind!' called Rasmussen, and he turned to see more Gallooniers and ball guests dropping from the side of the great vessel on ropes, in parachutes, and by any other means available. Stanley also caught a glimpse of Cloudier, being helped onto the deck of the Galloon by Clamdigger and Ms Huntley. He was glad to see that she was okay, but she didn't seem to be with the Brunt any more. The Captain and crew must have been working hard to bring the Galloon as low as possible, for now it was only a few dozen feet above the snowy slope.

Behind Stanley and Rasmussen, the busload of ball guests was preparing for battle. The Countess was giving a rousing speech, while around her, duchesses, butlers, waiters and lords did whatever they could to make ready. A selection of umbrellas, walking sticks and kitchen implements had been hastily handed round, and they were all being brandished in preparation for the forthcoming set-to. The charabanc wheeled and banked crazily, and Stanley felt a bump as it grazed the snowy slope, on its way to where the Sumbarooners were thickest. A sharp lump jumped to his throat as he realised that the focus of the Sumbarooners' attentions was a furry, growling bump in the snow – the Brunt!

Fishbane flew into the throng with his webbed talons whirling, and created enough of a gap for Stanley to see the Brunt, on all fours, seemingly cradling something to his chest, while fighting off the

Sumbarooners with one arm. They were shovelling snow onto him, and ripping off the last vestiges of his hot suit, and Stanley could see that his strength was failing.

'We've got to help him!' cried Rasmussen, who had been watching the same scene. They were now only a short distance away, and Hawthorne brought the charabanc to a skidding halt in the snow.

'Out, out, out, out!' shouted the Countess, helping passengers over the side of the charabanc, as Stanley and Rasmussen leapt free too.

'I'll go back for reinforcements!' cried Hawthorne, bringing the big bus round so that it faced down the slope.

'Bring rugs and blankets!' called Rasmussen, and Stanley understood her meaning immediately.

'And hot water bottles!' he cried, as he leapt away towards the Brunt, drawing his rusty little sword as he went.

Around them, the other contraptions were landing, floating to the ground, or otherwise entering the fray, and the tide of the fight was changing. Next to Stanley, the Sultana of Magrabor let fly a bloodcurdling war cry, and pulled a huge hatpin from her turban. The Countess of Hammerstein brandished her parasol round her head in a whirling parabola, and Little Ern rolled the spare wheel from the charabanc into the fray, where it knocked some Sumbarooners for six.

This gave Stanley the chance to jink through the crowd to the Brunt, who was now lying face down in the snow, both arms outstretched.

'Don't let them take it, Stanley,' he said weakly, before flopping down into the snow once more.

Stanley threw himself onto the Brunt, and wrapped his arms round one great leg, although he couldn't quite reach all the way round. Beside him, Rasmussen enveloped an arm, and they clung on tightly as the Sumbarooners continued to shovel snow onto them. Some of Zebediah's dastardly crew seemed to be intent on turning the Brunt over, which Stanley didn't understand the reason for at first. But as the Gallooniers around them began to engage the Sumbarooners in battle, he realised that their intent was to wrest from the Brunt whatever it was that he was clutching to his chest in one great hand. The Brunt seemed to be asleep again now, but at least the Gallooniers were beginning to win their fight to keep the enemy at bay.

'Keep him warm!' cried Stanley, as the Count of Eisberg leapt from a wobbling gyrocopter.

'We got your message!' he called back, as he fought off an iron-clad Sumbarooner with a tea tray and a candlestick. Wrapped round his waist was a thick blanket, and when he came close to where Stanley and

Rasmussen were clinging to the Brunt, he flung it to them. Stanley used it to wrap around one of the Brunt's legs, and as he looked round he saw that all the new arrivals to the fight were bringing rugs, blankets, hot water bottles and the like, which he and Rasmussen began to pile up on top of the Brunt.

Soon, the snow around him began to melt, and the attacking Sumbarooners began to melt away too, as it became clear that the fight was all but lost. More and more Gallooniers abseiled, flew and parachuted down from above, where the Galloon itself still hung like a solid thundercloud overhead.

The Brunt began to stir as the warmth returned to him, but Stanley knew the blankets would not be enough.

'We need to get him back onboard!' he called to Rasmussen, who was busy arranging hot water bottles around the Brunt's head.

They were now in the middle of a defensive ring – Gallooniers and ball guests were standing in a circle round the Brunt, keeping the Sumbarooners at bay with their improvised weaponry and dazzling skill. The flying vehicles were circling their heads, but Stanley knew that they could not get complacent.

Fishbane screeched past, and dropped a thick rope into the snow next to Stanley. The rope was coming from one of the flying machines. As they came close, each machine began dropping ropes, and Stanley and Rasmussen began tying these round the Brunt's great limbs. Beside them, Tarheel and Tamp appeared, and with their expertise in knotting, the Brunt was soon trussed up like a turkey, swaddled in blankets, and attached to the flotilla of flying contraptions by a net of ropes. The Sumbarooners were now standing off at a distance, trying to goad the Gallooniers into following them down the mountain, but Stanley was pleased to see that no one was biting. Reduced to flinging snowballs and abuse at the ring of stalwart Gallooniers, some Sumbarooners were starting to retreat. The Brunt was being lifted, carefully and slowly, from the snow, and was making stately progress up towards the Galloon. But would he get there quickly enough?

'They took it, Stanley! They took the token,' the Brunt called, as he shivered in the harness, and Stanley knew immediately what he was talking about.

'The Captain's love token! They found it, but the Brunt couldn't hold onto it!' he yelled at Rasmussen over the noise of the battle and the circling machines.

'For the Galloon!' shouted the Countess, who had overheard him.

'And for the Captain!' cried Snivens the butler, who had been in the thick of the battle throughout.

With a leap and yell, the entire company of

Gallooniers, from stable girls to minor royalty, began to rush down the mountainside towards the Sumbarooners. Stanley was distraught to see that Zebediah's men had a hefty lead, and that one of them, a tall thin woman in black, was waving a golden necklace above her head in triumph. At that moment, Stanley felt a pricking sensation as something grabbed hold of his shoulders. Looking up, he saw Fishbane the Seagle, his hooked beak just inches from Stanley's face, his talons holding tight to Stanley's jacket.

'No!' called Stanley. 'I need to be down there!'

But Fishbane was having none of it. Stanley watched the rush of battle from afar, as the Galloon's company routed Zebediah's men, but it was with a heavy heart that he was borne away, and back to the safety of the Galloon.

A half-hour or so later, Stanley was standing on the deck of the Great Galloon, where Cloudier now sat, blankets round her shoulders, drinking hot tea and warming her hands at a brazier. Clamdigger stood awkwardly behind her, as if unsure what to do with his arms. The Bilgepump Orchestra was still playing, but other than that, all semblance of a party was over. The Brunt lay on the deck, surrounded by braziers, under a pile of blankets, onto which Gallooniers were now piling yet more hot water bottles, bedpans and rugs. Ms Huntley was standing with Cloudier, and even Skyman Abel was making himself useful, handing out mugs of tea to the frozen warriors as they returned from the battle down below, while telling everyone what a vital role he had played, by staying on deck.

'The Galloon needed guarding, you see, a terribly dangerous job, but someone had to do it, and as usual it fell to me . . .'

Stanley knew that for once there was some truth in Abel's boasts – it was Abel, the Captain and Ms Huntley, along with a skeleton crew of brave Gallooniers, who had kept the Galloon safe, a few dozen people doing the job of hundreds, as most of the Gallooniers were overboard on the mountainside. Between them they had kept the Galloon rock steady, trimming sails, heaving at the wheel and manning the huge burners that let air into the network of balloons. It must have been a gargantuan task.

Yet the mood onboard was sombre. Everybody was aware that their whole quest had been for nought. Fishbane reported that the Sumbaroon had been seen limping out of the mouth of the cave, broken and bent but not destroyed. The Sumbarooners had returned to it in their flotilla of little boats, with the Captain's love token in their possession. The Galloon had stayed put, of course, as many of the Gallooniers were still on the mountainside, but Stanley knew it must have hurt the Captain immensely to let his brother get away. The Brunt's heroics, Cloudier's long journey, even the whole business with Fassbinder and the Grand Winter Ball, had all been for nought. The Captain was no closer to regaining the pendant, with its secret that was fundamental to the Galloon's future. And Zebediah had once again got away scot-free.

The last of the Gallooniers were now returning to the deck, including Rasmussen, who was perched in the cockpit of the gyrocopter. She was just about the only crewmember still smiling, and Stanley put this down to her joy at being flown about in all these fabulous machines. As the 'copter sputtered to a halt on the deck, Stanley was distracted by the arrival of the Captain himself, who was riding towards them in the back of a dog cart much like Clamdigger's. The Gallooniers, most of whom were milling about on deck, turned to look at him as he approached Cloudier. Stanley was surprised to see a broad smile crack the Captain's face as he held out a hand to her.

'I'm so relieved to see you well. I owe you everything,' he said to her, simply. Stanley thought he even heard a slight crack in the booming voice.

'But . . . we didn't get the love token,' said Cloudier, looking to where the Brunt lay under his pile of blankets.

'Not through want of trying,' said the Captain. 'Your

actions were an example to us all. If we had such a system in place, I would promote you forthwith.'

Cloudier smiled weakly, and Skyman Abel spluttered into his tea, as the Captain continued, turning now to the whole deck.

'Once again, I owe you all my thanks and my apologies. I have let my own priorities put my loyal friends at risk. We shall continue to chase down the Sumbaroon, of course we will. But first we will return to Eisberg, where we will help my good friend the Count repair his home, and where those of you who wish to do so may disembark. No longer will I pressure anyone into assisting me on my personal quests.'

A hubbub of noise greeted this announcement, the gist of which seemed to Stanley to be that no one was ready to disembark just yet.

'We can't just let the Sumbaroon float away!' called a marquess, to a chorus of agreement.

'We're here now, you won't get rid of us that easily!' shouted a young woman in a black and white uniform.

'I am moved, truly,' said the Captain. 'But the responsibility I feel for you all . . .'

'Nonsense!' called a cut-glass voice that Stanley recognised as the Sultana of Magrabor. 'We're all grown-ups. Enough of this nonsense. Let's get the Brunt here down below, so he can warm up and get stoking again. Then we can chase down this no-good brother of yours, retrieve the pendant and convince Isabella she's with the wrong man!'

'Hear hear, Sultana of Magrabor!' called the Brunt, to a rousing cheer. He was now sitting up, with blankets round his shoulders and his arms wrapped round a red-hot brazier.

'Well, I'm moved, I really am . . .' said the Captain, who seemed genuinely unsure as to what to do for the best. It took the Countess of Hammerstein's typically no-nonsense attitude to help make things clear for him.

'Captain Meredith Anstruther. We are here because we want to be, and we help you because we are your friends. If you would please take that into account in future, I think we have a good chance of finding your stolen bride, and bringing her back to your side.'

With tears in his eyes, the Captain managed to croak, 'But . . . without the token, we're constantly at risk. And what . . . what if she doesn't believe me?'

'Of course she'll . . .' began Ms Huntley, with a tone of exasperation Stanley was getting used to hearing from her in her dealings with the Captain. But she didn't finish her sentence, as an ear-splitting whistle cut across the deck, emanating from the spot where Marianna Rasmussen sat on a water butt, swinging an item of jewellery from one nonchalant fist.

'Do you mean *this* lost love token?' she said, examining her nails in an infuriatingly offhand manner.

'Egad!' cried the Captain, as the noise level amongst the crowd swelled with excitement.

'Marianna Rasmussen!' cried the Countess. 'How on earth . . .?'

'Well,' said Rasmussen, with a slightly sheepish look on her face now. 'I may have . . . erm . . . swapped it for a priceless Hammerstein family heirloom necklace while we were trying to keep the Brunt warm in the snow . . .'

Stanley laughed out loud as he thought of the look on Zebediah's face when the triumphant Sumbarooners brought him a 'lost love token' in the shape of a bejewelled kitten-shaped compact on a golden chain.

'Sorry, Mother,' said Rasmussen, with a look of genuine contrition on her face that Stanley had never seen before.

'My dear, even if that compact had been worth as much as the Galloon itself, it would have been worth the swap.'

The Countess looked around, before appearing to make a decision.

'And besides,' she said, her head held proudly in the air. 'As it happens, I sold all the Hammerstein family heirlooms many years ago, to make ends meet. That compact was a piece of paste, nothing more. We are as poor as Little Ern here.'

'Oh I say!' cried Able Skyman Abel, but his shock was drowned out by a wave of laughter that swept around the crowd.

'You may be penniless, Birgit,' cried the Count of Eisberg, 'but you will never be poor – not while you have the Galloon and its people about you!'

This pronouncement was followed by an uproarious cheer. Rasmussen, slightly sickened by this cloying turn of events, but relieved to be off the hook, leapt down from where she sat and ran over to Mr Lungren, who stood watching the goings-on from his place by the band. She whispered in his ear, and he turned to the Orchestra. They struck up a lively dance number, and soon the party was in full swing again.

The Captain, who at first seemed dumbstruck by recent events, was soon to be seen dancing with all and sundry, the golden pendant gleaming round his neck as he twirled and leapt in a complicated ceilidh of joy. The Brunt stayed a short while, being slapped on the back, and sheepishly deflecting questions, but before too long he was seen sneaking back down the main hatchway, a brazier under each arm, on his way back to his hot little room and the home comforts he held so dear.

After a few dances, the Captain, sweeping stray hair

from his eyes, slumped down onto a chair next to where Stanley and Rasmussen sat eating cake.

'You know, you may well have saved the day once again, my young friends,' he said quietly.

'Well, it was quite easy really, swapping the necklaces . . .' began Rasmussen, but the Captain laid a steady hand on her arm as he continued.

'Not just that. If you hadn't kept an eye on Charlie, followed Fassbinder, made the Brunt warm in the snow, where would the Galloon be now? I owe you so much. Is there anything I can do for you?'

Astounded by this, Stanley and Rasmussen eyed each other.

'There is one thing you could tell us,' said Stanley warily.

'Go on,' said the Captain, taking a sip from a glass of hot punch.

'Why is the pendant vital to the future of the Galloon?' asked Stanley.

'Ah. A good question,' said the Captain, a serious look on his face now. 'I will show you why. Come.'

Stanley and Rasmussen followed him, the now familiar thrill of being alone with the Captain welling up in them. Together they hopped in a dog cart, and with the Captain's cry of 'mush!' they were soon trundling along the decks, towards the quarterdeck, where the Captain's wheelhouse stood. They felt the eyes of the partygoers on them as they trundled through the crowds. Once there, they hopped out and followed the Captain up a short ladder and into the wheelhouse itself – the hallowed inner sanctum, where neither of them had ever been before.

There was the great wheel of the Galloon, fully as broad as the Captain was tall, with brassbound handles sticking out from each huge spoke. It creaked and moved slightly as the Galloon pulled at its moorings.

'Try and move the wheel,' said the Captain calmly.

Stanley looked at Rasmussen, who shrugged a little, then he stepped up to the wheel and reached for the nearest handle.

CLANG.

A metal cage or grating, like a huge iron gate, shot up from the floor and covered the wheel entirely. Stanley stepped back, and – CLANG – it fell back into the floor. He stepped up again, and CLANG.

There was the grating, stopping him getting within two or three feet of the wheel and the other controls. As Stanley watched, the grating began to heat up, until it was cherry red all over.

'How do you . . .?' said Rasmussen, bemused.

'There is a code,' said the Captain, clearly pleased to be able to tell someone all this. He turned round, to where eight brass levers stuck up from the floor, each one about five feet tall.

'To be allowed access to the wheel, these levers must be set in a precise configuration – different each day of the year, dependent on the seasons, the tides, the movement of the stars, and the current price of a cup of tea in the mess. I carry this information in my head – but I cannot be the only person who knows. What if something were to happen to me?'

'But what . . .' said Stanley, although realisation was beginning to dawn.

'The pendant!' said Rasmussen. 'Those patterns on the back – it's not just a pretty design. It's the key to the code!'

'The legend. I intended for Isabella to have both parts, once we were married. But it never got that far.'

'So – if Zebediah got hold of the pendant, he could fly the Galloon,' said Stanley.

'He'd have to get past me first, and make it up here to the wheelhouse, but yes. His chances would be much improved. But Isabella's half of the token only contains half of the legend – useless on its own.'

'So that's why retrieving the token was so important!' said Rasmussen, almost as if she was relieved to know that all this trouble had not been taken in vain.

'What's important is that we are all here, we are all well, and we all live to fight another day. But I will not ask you to risk your lives for me again. While you were down there, fighting so gallantly for the Brunt, and the token, and the Great Galloon, I was beginning to teach the vagaries of this machine to Ms Huntley. Soon I will no longer be the only person able to fly it.'

'But we still need to find Isabella,' said Rasmussen. 'They could be miles away by now, if they've managed to fix the Sumbaroon.'

'Oh yes, even the Kraken's attack will not have slowed up my brother's departure. He will be far away before long. If only there were some way of finding out what was happening onboard his infernal Sumbaroon from a distance. Then we would have the advantage we need . . .' said the Captain, deep in thought once more.

Stanley looked again at Rasmussen, who raised an eyebrow knowingly.

'Let's just enjoy the party for now . . .' he signed to her, surreptitiously, in the secret sign language that only they knew.

'Cloudy with a chance of rain I believe, but I don't see the relevance of that right now . . .' she replied irritably.

He rolled his eyes, and together they went off to dance.

*　　*　　*

Far below, in the cosy cabin Stanley shared with his pet rat, a mysterious black box buzzed into life. Written on the front was the following phrase:

The Long-Distance Examinator
Invented by T. Crumplehorn.
Property of Stanley Crumplehorn, for the purpose of learning lessons and keeping in touch.

A light flashed on the front of the box, and a dial twirled of its own accord. A crackling noise trickled from the single speaker, causing the rat to sit up in his bed of straw, and nibble a nut excitedly.

'. . . body out there . . .?' said a disembodied voice, causing the rat to drop its nut and listen.

The machine crackled again, then a kind of metallic, echoing 'ping' noise took the place of the speech for a few moments.

'. . . hear us?' said the same voice after a pause, followed by a different person saying, 'If you can hear us, give us a sign . . .?'

'Testing . . . testing . . .' said the first voice, that of a boy of around ten, before continuing. 'No use . . . if there was anyone out there, they'd need a machine of their own to be able to hear us . . .'

'I know,' said the second voice, a girl of about the same age. 'But if we've made one, surely there's a chance . . .' The crackling took over again, and the voices died out, to be replaced by someone singing in a foreign language, then part of a weather report.

The rat went back to sleep again, so even he didn't hear the last few words that came from the Long-Distance Examinator.

'If anyone is listening, we'd love to hear from you . . . call us back . . . using the call sign "Grand Sumbaroon" . . . this is Big Dipper, signing off, from the Grand Sumbaroon . . .'

'Told you . . .' said the girl's voice, slightly petulantly. 'Useless. Now, can we please go and find an adventure of some sort . . .'

The Sultana of Magrabor's Splendiferous Etiquette and Gallooning Quizzette

Write in fine black ink on high-quality paper only, please. None of this cheap muck. Smugness will not be tolerated. Anyone scoring above eighty per cent will be downgraded for being too clever by half. You may turn your papers over . . . wait for it . . . NOW!

Q1. How should one correctly address myself, the Sultana of Magrabor?

   a) Harness of the Four Winds

   b) Empress of the Lowest Lands

   c) Wearer of the Biggest Pantson

Q2. What do I, the Sultana of Magrabor, usually wear on my head?

   a) A turban

   b) A turbot

   c) A pair of pants

Q3. In *Voyage to the Volcano*, mention is made of a charabanc (pronounced 'sharrabang'). What is a charabanc?

   a) A vegetable, similar to a carrot but with the temperament of a rattlesnake

b) A type of old-fashioned open-topped bus
c) A pair of pants

Q4. The automaton Fassbinder is unmasked in *Voyage to the Volcano*. Which part of him sends a warning signal to Zebediah in his final moments?

a) His eye, which sprouts an aerial and floats in the air
b) His leg, which hops overboard and swims to safety
c) His pants, which let off a hideous warning stink

Q5. What is the name of the Volcano where Cloudier and the Brunt find the Captain's love token?

a) The Kraken's Stair
b) The Kraken's Lair
c) The Kraken's Pair . . . of Pants

Mark your answers clearly, fold the paper carefully, place it in an envelope made of lead, and then drop it in the sea, as far as I'm concerned. I don't give a monkey's whether you got the questions right or not. Life's too short for such things. I've never done a test in my life, and look where I am today. Let's have a dance, shall we?

Erm – Sultana, I think we should at least give them the answers, if you don't mind.

Captain A.

Ah. Yes, of course, Captain. Only joking, of course. So:

Q1. a) or b) are correct, although c) is perfectly true. They're quite enormous.

Q2. a). I wear a turban, although I have worn a turbot once, when I went to a fancy-dress party dressed as the sea floor. As well as the turbot, I had a seashell bra and a sandy bottom. Happy days.

Q3. It's b). I've never known a vegetable with the temperament of a rattlesnake. Although I did once eat a parsnip that didn't agree with me.

Q4. a) It's his eye that pops out and sends off a signal. His pants were, as far as we know, squeaky clean.

Q5. As Kraken means 'whale', it's very unlikely that any of them would wear pants – you just can't get them in big enough sizes, and I should know. So the answer is b), the Kraken's Lair.

Well done – if any of you got all the questions right, you can consider yourselves experts on the affair of the Kraken's Lair. If any of you answered 'Pants' to all the questions, you can consider yourselves experts in knowing what's funny and what isn't. If any of you got them all wrong, go back and try again now you know the answers. If you still get them all wrong, you really need to start paying more attention.